THE
MILLIONAIRE
AND THE MAID

THE MILLIONAIRE AND THE MAID

BY

MICHELLE DOUGLAS

WARWICKSHIRE
COUNTY LIBRARY

CONTROL No.

MILLS
BOON

All rights reserved including the right of reproduction
in whole or in part in any form. This edition is published
by arrangement with Harlequin Books S.A.

This is a work of fiction. Names, characters, places,
locations and incidents are purely fictional and bear
no relationship to any real life individuals, living or
dead, or to any actual places, business establishments,
locations, events or incidents. Any resemblance is entirely
coincidental.

This book is sold subject to the condition that it shall not,
by way of trade or otherwise, be lent, resold, hired out
or otherwise circulated without the prior consent of the
publisher in any form of binding or cover other than that
in which it is published and without a similar condition
including this condition being imposed on the subsequent
purchaser.

® and TM are trademarks owned and used by the
trademark owner and/or its licensee. Trademarks
marked with ® are registered with the United Kingdom
Patent Office and/or the Office for Harmonisation in the
Internal Market and in other countries.

First published in Great Britain 2015
by Mills & Boon, an imprint of Harlequin (UK) Limited,
Large Print edition 2015
Eton House, 18-24 Paradise Road,
Richmond, Surrey, TW9 1SR

© 2015 Michelle Douglas

ISBN: 978-0-263-25666-6

Harlequin (UK) Limited's policy is to use papers that
are natural, renewable and recyclable products and made
from wood grown in sustainable forests. The logging
and manufacturing processes conform to the legal
environmental regulations of the country of origin.

Printed and bound in Great Britain
by CPI Antony Rowe, Chippenham, Wiltshire

To Laurie Johnson for her enthusiasm,
insight…and for introducing me to mojitos.
It was a joy to work with you.

CHAPTER ONE

MAC PRESSED THE heels of his hands to his eyes and counted to five before pulling them away and focussing on the computer screen again. He reread what he'd written of the recipe so far and fisted his hands. *What came next?*

This steamed mussels dish was complicated, but he must have made it a hundred times. He ground his teeth together. The words blurred and danced across the screen. Why couldn't he remember what came next?

Was it coconut milk?

He shook his head. That came later.

With a curse, he leapt up, paced across the room and tried to imagine making the dish. He visualised himself in a kitchen, with all the ingredients arrayed around him. He imagined speaking directly to a rolling camera to explain what he was doing—the necessity of each ingredient and the importance of the sequence. His chest swelled and then cramped. He dragged a hand back through his hair. To be cooking…to be back at work… A black well of longing rose through him, drowning him with a need so great he thought the darkness would swallow him whole.

It'd be a blessing if it did.

Except he had work to do.

He kicked out at a pile of dirty washing bunched in the corner of the room before striding back to his desk and reaching for the bottle of bourbon on the floor beside it. It helped to blunt the pain. For a little while. He lifted it to his mouth and then halted. The heavy curtains drawn at the full-length windows blocked the sunlight from the room, and while his body had no idea—it was in a seemingly permanent state of jet lag—his brain told him it was morning.

Grinding his teeth, he screwed the cap back on the bottle.

Finish the damn recipe. Then you can drink yourself into oblivion and sleep.

Finish the recipe? That was what he had to do, but he couldn't seem to turn from where he stood, staring at the closed curtains, picturing the day just beyond them, the sun and the light and the cool of the fresh air…the smell of the sea.

He kept himself shut away from all that temptation.

But it didn't stop him from being able to imagine it.

A ping from his computer broke the spell. Dragging a hand down his face, he turned back to the desk and forced himself into the chair.

A message. From Russ. Of course. It was always Russ. Just for a moment he rested his head in his hands.

Hey Bro, don't forget Jo arrives today.

He swore. He didn't need a housekeeper. He needed peace and quiet so he could finish this damn cookbook.

If the rotten woman hadn't saved his brother's life he'd send her off with a flea in her ear.

Scrubbing a hand through his hair, he shook that thought off. He understood the need to retreat from the world. He wouldn't begrudge that to someone else. He and this housekeeper—they wouldn't have to spend any time in each other's company. In fact they wouldn't even need to come face to face. He'd left her a set of written instructions on the kitchen table. As for the rest she could please herself.

He planted himself more solidly in his chair,

switched off his internet connection, and shut the siren call of sunshine, fresh air and living from his mind. He stared at the screen.

Add the chilli purée and clam broth and reduce by a half. Then add…

What the hell came next?

Jo pushed out of her car and tried to decide what to look at first—the view or the house. She'd had to negotiate for two rather hairy minutes over a deeply rutted driveway. It had made her grateful that her car was a four-wheel drive, equipped to deal with rough terrain, rather than the sports car her soul secretly hungered for. After five hours on the road she was glad to have reached her destination. Still, five hours in a sports car would have been more fun.

She shook out her arms and legs. *'You can't put her in that! She's too big-boned.'* Her great-aunt's voice sounded through her mind. She half laughed. True, she'd probably look ridiculous in a sport car. Besides, what were the odds that she wouldn't even fit into one? As ever, though, her grandmother's voice piped up. *'I think she looks pretty and I don't care what anyone else thinks.'*

With a shake of her head, Jo shut out the duelling voices. She'd work out a plan of attack for Grandma and Great-Aunt Edith later. Instead, she moved out further onto the bluff to stare at the view. In front of her the land descended sharply to a grassy field that levelled out before coming to a halt at low, flower-covered sand dunes. Beyond that stretched a long crescent of deserted beach, glittering white-gold in the mild winter sunlight.

A sigh eased out of her. There must be at least six or seven kilometres of it—two to the left and four or five to the right—and not a soul to be seen. All the way along it perfect blue-green breakers rolled up to the shore in a froth of white.

She sucked a breath of salt-laced air into her lungs and some of the tension slipped out of her. With such a vast expanse of ocean in front of her, her own troubles seemed suddenly less significant. Not that she had troubles as such. Just a few things she needed to sort out.

She dragged in another breath. The rhythmic whooshing of the waves and the cries of two seagulls cruising overhead eased the knots five hours in the car had conspired to create. The green of each wave as it crested made her inhalations come more easily, as if the push and pull of the

Pacific Ocean had attuned her breathing to a more natural pattern.

The breeze held a chill she found cleansing. Last week the weather would have been warm enough to swim, and maybe it'd be warm enough for that again next week. Having spent the last eight years working in the Outback, she hadn't realised how much she'd missed the coast and the beach.

She finally turned to survey the house. A two-storey weatherboard with a deep veranda and an upstairs balcony greeted her. A lovely breezy home that—

She frowned at all the closed windows and drawn curtains, the shut front door. Heavens, Mac MacCallum *was* still here, wasn't he? Russ would have told her if his brother had returned to the city.

She sucked her bottom lip into her mouth and then folded her arms. Mac would be in there. Russ had warned her that his brother might prove difficult. He'd also had no doubt in her ability to handle difficult.

'Jeez, you save someone's life and suddenly they think you're Superwoman.'

But she'd smiled as she'd said it—though whether in affection at her dear friend and former boss, or at the thought of wearing a superhero outfit she wasn't sure. Though if she burst in wearing a spangly leotard and cape it might make Mac reconsider the soundness of locking himself away like this.

She planted her hands on her hips.

Painted a sleek grey, each weatherboard sat in perfect alignment with its neighbour—and, considering the battering the place must take from sand, salt, sun and wind, that was a testament to the superior materials used and to whoever had built it. The best that money could buy, no doubt. The galvanised tin roof shone in the sunlight. There was even a chimney, which must mean there was an open fire. *Nice!* Winter might be relatively mild here on the mid-north coast of New South Wales, but she didn't doubt the nights could be chilly.

She pulled her cardigan about her more tightly. Still, shut up as it was, the house looked cold and unwelcoming even in all this glorious sunshine.

There's only one way to change that.

Casting a final longing glance back behind her, she set her shoulders and strode towards the house, mounting the six steps to the veranda two at a time.

A piece of paper, stark white against the grey wood, was taped to the door with *'Ms Anderson'* slashed across it in a dark felt-tipped pen. Jo peeled the note away. Was Mac out? And was he going to insist on the formality of 'Ms Anderson' and 'Mr MacCallum'?

Ms Anderson
   I don't like to be disturbed while I'm working so let yourself in. Your room is on the ground floor beyond the kitchen. There should be absolutely no need for you to venture up onto the first floor.

She let out a low laugh. Oh, so that was what he thought, huh?

He finished with:

   I eat at seven. Please leave a tray on the table at the bottom of the stairs and I'll collect it when I take a break from my work.

She folded the note and shoved it in her pocket. She opened the front door and propped a cast-iron rooster that she assumed to be the doorstop against it, and then latched the screen door back against the house before going to the car and collecting her cases. And then she strode into the house as if she owned it—head high, shoulders back, spine straight.

Malcolm 'Mac' MacCallum had another think

coming if he thought they were going to spend the next two months or so communicating via notes.

She dropped her suitcases in the hallway, wrinkling her nose at the musty scent of old air and neglect. A large reception room lay to her right. She strode in and flung open the curtains at the three large windows to let light spill into the room. She turned and blew out a breath.

Look at all this gorgeous furniture.

Antiques mingled with newer pieces, creating an elegant warmth that reminded her again of Mac's success. She glared at a gorgeous leather chair. What use was success if it made you forget the people who loved you? Mac hadn't visited Russ once since Russ's heart attack. She transferred her glare to the ceiling, before shaking herself and glancing around the room again. It was all in serious need of spit and polish.

She grimaced. Tomorrow.

She turned her back on it to open the windows. The sound of the sea entered first, and then its scent. She straightened. That was better.

She found her room at the back of the house. Someone had made a half-hearted effort at cleaning it. Mac, she supposed. According to Russ, the last cleaning lady had left over a month ago.

It would do for now. She'd tackle that tomorrow as well.

Her window looked out over an unkempt lawn to a garage. She lifted the window higher. She might not have a room with a view, but she could still hear the ocean. She leant against the window-sill, reaching out to touch a banksia flower on the nearby tree.

A moment later she drew her hand back, a breath shuddering out of her as she thought back to that stupid note stuck to the door. Perhaps this wasn't such a good idea. Turning her life upside down like this was probably foolhardy, irresponsible—even insane. After all, geology wasn't so bad and—

It's not so good either.

She bit her lip and then straightened. She'd gone into geology to please her father. For all the good it had done her. She wasn't concerned with pleasing him any longer.

She'd remained in the field to keep the peace. She didn't want just to keep the peace any more—she wanted to create a new world where peace reigned…at least in her little part of it. She'd stayed where she was because she was frightened of change. Well, Russ's heart attack had taught her that there were worse things than fear of change.

Fear of regret and fear of wasting her life were two of those things. She couldn't afford to lose heart now. She wanted a future she could look forward to. She wanted a future that would make her proud. She wanted a future that mattered. That was what she was doing here. That wasn't foolhardy, irresponsible or insane. On the contrary.

But…what about Mac? What was she going to do? Follow instructions today and then try to corner him tomorrow? Or—?

Her phone buzzed in her pocket. She glanced at the caller ID before lifting it to her ear. 'Hey, Russ.'

'Are you there yet?'

'Yep.'

'How's Mac?'

She swallowed. *Or not follow instructions?*

'I've only just this very minute arrived, so I haven't clapped eyes on him yet, but let me tell you the view here is amazing. Your brother has found the perfect place to…'

What? Recuperate? He'd had enough time to recuperate. Work without distractions? Hole up?

'The perfect place to hide away from the world.' Russell sighed.

Russ was fifty-two and recovering from a heart attack. He was scheduled for bypass surgery in a few weeks. She wasn't adding to his stress if she could help it.

'The perfect place for inspiration,' she countered. 'The scenery is gorgeous. Wait until you see it and then you'll know what I mean. I'll send you photos.'

'Does a body need inspiration to write a cookbook?'

She had no idea. 'Cooking and making up recipes are creative endeavours, aren't they? And isn't there some theory that creativity is boosted by the negative ions of moving water? Anyway, there's lots of deserted beach to walk and rolling hills to climb. It's a good place to come and get strong—away from prying eyes.'

'You think so?'

'Absolutely. Give me an hour, Russ, and I'll call you back when I have something concrete to tell you, okay?'

'I can't thank you enough for doing this, Jo.'

'We both know that in this instance it's you who's doing me the favour.'

It wasn't wholly a lie.

She'd known Russ for eight years. They'd hit if off from the first day she'd walked into the mining company's Outback office, with her brand-new soil sample kit and her work boots that still held a shine. Their teasing, easy rapport had developed into a genuine friendship. He'd been her boss, her mentor, and one of the best friends she'd ever had—but in all that time she'd never met his brother.

After his heart attack she'd confided in Russ— told him she wanted out of geology and away from the Outback. She grimaced. She'd also told him she couldn't go back to Sydney until she'd developed a plan. Her jobless situation would only provide Grandma and Great-Aunt Edith with more ammunition to continue their silly feud. Battle lines would be drawn and Jo would find herself smack-bang in the middle of them. She was already smack-bang in the middle of them! No more. She was tired of living her life to meet other people's expectations.

She pulled in a breath. When she was working in a job she loved and doing things that made her happy, the people who loved her—Grandma and Great-Aunt Edith—would be happy for her too. She squinted out of the window. If only she could figure out what it was that would make her happy.

She chafed her arms, suddenly cold. All she knew was that another twenty years down the track she didn't want to look back and feel she'd wasted her life.

When Russ had found all that out he'd laughed and rubbed his hands together. 'Jo,' he'd said, 'I've just the job for you.'

And here she was.

She glanced around, her nose wrinkling.

She loved Russ dearly. She enjoyed his twisted sense of humour, admired the values he upheld, and she respected the man he was. She did not, however, hold out the same hopes for his brother.

She planted her hands on her hips. A brother did not desert his family when they needed him. Russ had been there for Mac every step of the way, but Mac had been nowhere to be found when Russ had needed him. But here she was, all the same. Mac's hired help. She didn't even know what her official job title was—cook, cleaner, housekeeper? Russ had dared her to don a French maid's outfit. Not in this lifetime!

Russ needed someone to make sure Mac was getting three square meals a day and not living in squalor—someone who could be trusted not to go racing to the press. At heart, though, Jo knew Russ just wanted to make sure his little brother was okay.

Cue Jo. Still, this job would provide her with the peace and quiet to work out where she wanted to go from here.

She pulled Mac's note from her pocket and stared at it.

There should be absolutely no reason for you to venture onto the first floor.

Oh, yes, there was.

Without giving herself too much time to think, she headed straight for the stairs.

There were five doors on the first floor, if she didn't count the door to the linen closet. Four of them stood wide open—a bathroom and three bedrooms. Mind you, all the curtains in each of those rooms were drawn, so it was dark as Hades up here. The fourth door stood resolutely closed. *Do Not Disturb* vibes radiated from it in powerful waves.

'Guess which one the prize is behind?' she murmured under her breath, striding up to it.

She lifted her hand and knocked. *Rat-tat-tat!* The noise bounced up and down the hallway. No answer. Nothing.

She knocked again, even louder. 'Mac, are you in there?'

To hell with calling him Mr MacCallum. Every Tuesday night for the last five years she'd sat with Russ, watching Mac on the television. For eight years she'd listened to Russ talk about his brother. He would be Mac to her forever.

She suddenly stiffened. What if he was hurt or sick?

'Go away!'

She rolled her eyes. '"There was movement at the station."'

'Can't you follow instructions?'

Ooh, that was a veritable growl. 'I'm afraid not. I'm coming in.'

She pushed the door open.

'What the hell?' The single light at the desk was immediately clicked off. 'Get out! I told you I didn't want to be disturbed.'

'Correction. An anonymous note informed me that someone didn't want to be disturbed.' It took a moment for her eyes to adjust to the darkness. She focussed on that rather than the snarl in his voice. 'Anyone could've left that note. For all I knew you could've been slain while you slept.'

He threw his arms out. 'Not slain. See? Now, get out.'

'I'd like nothing better,' she said, strolling across the room.

'What the hell do you think you're—?'

He broke off when she flung the curtains back. She pulled in a breath, staring at the newly revealed balcony and the magnificent view beyond. 'Getting a good look at you,' she said, before turning around.

The sight that met her shocked her to the core. She had no hope of hiding it. She reached out a hand to steady herself against the glass doors.

'Happy?'

His lips twisted in a snarl that made her want to flee. She swallowed and shook her head. 'No.' How could she be happy? He was going to break his brother's heart.

'Shocked?' he mocked with an ugly twist of his lips.

The left side of his face and neck were red, tight and raw with the post-burn scarring from his accident. His too-long blond hair had clumped in greasy unbrushed strands. Dark circles rimmed red eyes. The grey pallor of his skin made her stomach churn.

'To the marrow,' she choked out.

And in her mind the first lines of that Banjo Paterson poem went round and round in her head.

There was movement at the station,
for the word had passed around
That the colt from old Regret had got away

Regret. Got away. She suddenly wished with everything inside her that *she* could get away. Leave.

And go where? What would she tell Russ?

She swallowed and straightened. 'It smells dreadful in here.'

Too close and sour and hot. She slid the door open, letting the sea breeze dance over her. She filled her lungs with it even though his scowl deepened.

'I promised Russ I'd clap eyes on you, as no one else seems to have done so in months.'

'He sent you here as a spy?'

'He sent me here as a favour.'

'I don't need any favours!'

Not a favour for you. But she didn't say that out loud. 'No. I suspect what you really need is a psychiatrist.'

His jaw dropped.

She pulled herself up to her full height of six feet and folded her arms. 'Is that what you *really* want me to report back to Russ? That you're in a deep depression and possibly suicidal?'

His lips drew together tightly over his teeth. 'I am neither suicidal nor depressed.'

'Right.' She drew the word out, injecting as much disbelief into her voice as she could. 'For the last four months you've sat shut up in this dark house, refusing to see a soul. I suspect you barely sleep and barely eat.' She wrinkled her nose. 'And when was the last time you had a shower?'

His head rocked back.

'These are not the actions of a reasonable or rational adult. What interpretation would you put on them if you were coming in from the outside? What conclusion do you think Russ would come to?'

For a moment she thought he might have paled at her words—except he was already so pale it was impossible to tell. She rubbed a hand across her chest. She understood that one had to guard against sunburn on burn scars, but avoiding the light completely was ludicrous.

He said nothing. He just stared at her as if seeing her for the first time. Which just went to show how preoccupied he must have been. When most people saw her for the first time they usually performed a comical kind of double-take at her sheer size. Not that she'd ever found anything remotely humorous about it. So what? She was tall. And, no, she wasn't dainty. It didn't make her a circus freak.

'Damn you, Mac!' She found herself shouting at him, and she didn't know where it came from but it refused to be suppressed. 'How can you be so selfish? Russell is recovering from a heart attack. He needs bypass surgery. He needs calm and peace and...' Her heart dropped with a sickening thud. 'And now I'm going to have to tell him...' She faltered, not wanting to put into words Mac's pitiable condition. She didn't have the heart for it.

Mac still didn't speak, even though the ferocity and outrage had drained from his face. She shook her head and made for the door.

'At least I didn't waste any time unpacking.'

It wasn't until the woman— What was her name again? Jo Anderson? It wasn't until she'd disappeared through his bedroom door that he realised what she meant to do.

She meant to leave.

She meant to leave and tell Russ that Mac needed to be sectioned or something daft. Hell, the press would have a field-day with *that*! But she was right about one thing—Russ didn't need the added stress of worrying about Mac. Mac had enough guilt on that head as it was, and he wasn't adding to it.

'Wait!' he hollered.

He bolted after her, hurling himself down the stairs, knocking into walls and stumbling, his body heavy and unfamiliar as if it didn't belong to him any more. By the time he reached the bottom he was breathing hard.

He'd used to jog five kilometres without breaking a sweat.

When was the last time he'd jogged?

When was the last time you had a shower?

He dragged a hand down his face. God help him.

He shook himself back into action and surged forward, reaching the front door just as she lugged her cases down the front steps. Sunlight. Sea air. He pulled up as both pounded at him, caressing him, mocking him. He didn't want to notice how good they felt. But they felt better than good.

And they'd both distract him from his work. *Work you won't get a chance to complete if Jo Anderson walks away.*

He forced himself forward, through the door. 'Please, Ms Anderson—wait.'

She didn't stop. The woman was built like an

Amazon—tall and regal. It hurt him to witness the fluid grace and elegance of her movements. In the same way the sunlight and the sea breeze hurt him. It hurt him to witness her strength and the tilt of her chin and the dark glossiness of her hair.

Jo Anderson was, quite simply, stunning. Like the sunlight and the sea breeze. There was something just as elemental about her, and it made him not want to mess with her, but he had to get her to stop. And that meant messing with her.

With his heart thumping, he forced himself across the veranda until he stood fully in the sun. His face started to burn. The burning wasn't real, but being outside made him feel exposed and vulnerable. He forced himself down the steps.

'Jo, please don't leave.'

She stopped at his use of her first name.

Say something that will make her lower her cases to the ground.

His heart hammered and his mouth dried as the breeze seared across his skin. It took all his strength not to flinch as the sun warmed his face. He dragged a breath of air into his lungs—fresh sea air—and it provided him with the answer he needed.

'I'm sorry.'

He sent up a prayer of thanks when she lowered her cases and turned. 'Are you really? I suspect you're merely sorry someone's called you on whatever game it is you've been playing.'

Game? *Game!* He closed his eyes and reined in his temper. He couldn't afford to alienate her further.

'Please don't take tales back to Russ that will cause him worry. He…he needs… He doesn't need the stress.'

She stared at him. She had eyes the colour of sage. He briefly wondered if sage was the elusive ingredient he'd been searching for all morning, before shaking the thought away.

Jo tilted her chin and narrowed her eyes. 'I don't take anyone's wellbeing or health for granted, Mac. Not any more. And—'

'This is *my* life we're talking about,' he cut in. 'Don't I get any say in the matter?'

'I'd treat you like an adult if you'd been acting like one.'

'You can't make that judgement based on five minutes' acquaintance. I've been having a *very* bad day.' He widened his stance. 'What do I need to do to convince you that I am, in fact, neither depressed nor suicidal?'

He would not let her go worrying Russ with this. He would *not* be responsible for physically harming yet another person.

She folded her arms and stuck out a hip—a rather lush, curvaceous hip—and a pulse started up deep inside him.

'What do you need to do to convince me? Oh, Mac, that's going to take some doing.'

Her voice washed over him like warm honey. It was a warmth that didn't sting.

For no reason at all his pulse kicked up a notch. He envied her vigour and conviction. She stalked up to him to peer into his face. To try to read his motives, he suspected. She was only an inch or two shorter than him, and she smelt like freshly baked bread. His mouth watered.

Then he recalled the look in her eyes when she'd recovered from her first sight of him and he angled the left side of his face away from her. Her horror hadn't dissolved into pity—which was something, he supposed. It had been scorn. Her charge of selfishness had cut through to his very marrow, slicing through the hard shell of his guilt and anger.

'Stay for a week,' he found himself pleading.

His mouth twisted. Once upon a time he'd been able to wrap any woman around his little finger.

He'd flash a slow smile or a cheeky grin and don the charm. He suspected that wouldn't work on this woman. Not now. And not back then, when he'd still been pretty, either.

Mind you, it seemed he'd lost his charm at about the same time he'd lost his looks. Now he looked like a monster.

It doesn't mean you have to act like one, though.

Her low laugh drizzled over him like the syrup for his Greek lemon cake.

'I believe you're serious…'

Yeah? Well, at the very least it'd buy Russ another week of rest and—

What the hell? This woman didn't know him from Adam. She had no idea what he was capable of. He pulled himself upright—fully upright—and the stretch felt good.

'Name your price.'

He wasn't sure if it was more scorn or humour that flitted through her eyes. She straightened too, but he still had a good two inches on her. She could try and push him around all she wanted. He—

He grimaced. Yeah, well, if he didn't want her worrying Russ she *could* push him around. Whoever happened to be bigger in this particular scenario didn't make a scrap of difference.

He thrust out his chin. Still, he *was* bigger.

'Name my price?'

He swallowed. She had a voice made for radio—a kind of solid-gold croon that would soothe any angry beast.

'Well, for a start I'd want to see you exercising daily.'

It took a moment for the import of her words rather than their sound to reach him.

Risk being seen in public? *No!* He—

'During daylight hours,' she continued remorselessly. 'You need vitamin D and to lose that awful pallor.'

'You do know I've been ill, don't you?' he demanded. 'That I've been in hospital?'

'You haven't been in hospital for months. Do you have *any* idea how much you've let yourself go? You used to have a strong, lean body and lovely broad shoulders.'

Which were still broader than hers. Though he didn't point that out.

'And you used to move with a lanky, easy saunter. Now…? Now you look about fifty.'

He glared. He was only forty.

'And not a good fifty either. You look as if I could snap you in half.'

He narrowed his eyes. 'I wouldn't advise you to try that.'

She blinked and something chased itself across her face, as if she'd suddenly realised he was a man—a living, breathing man—rather than a job or a problem she had to solve.

Not that it meant she fancied him or anything stupid like that. How could anyone fancy him now? But...

For the first time since the fire he suddenly *felt* like a living, breathing man.

'If you want me to change my mind about you, Mac, I want to see you walk down to the beach and back every day. It's all your own property, so you don't need to be worried about bumping into strangers if you're that jealous of your privacy.'

'The beach is public land.' He had neighbours who walked on it every day.

'I didn't say you had to walk *along* it—just down to it.'

'The land that adjoins my property to the north—' he gestured to the left '—is all national park.' There'd be the occasional hiker.

'So walk along that side of your land, then.' She gestured to the right and then folded her arms. 'I'm simply answering your question. If you find daily exercise too difficult, then I've probably made my point.'

He clenched his jaw, breathed in for the count of five and then unclenched it to ask, 'What else?'

'I'd like you to separate your work and sleep areas. A defined routine to your day will help me believe you have a handle on things. Hence a work-space that's separate from your bedroom.'

He glared at her. 'Fine—whatever. And...?'

'I'd also want you to give up alcohol. Or at least drinking bourbon in your room on your own.'

She'd seen the bottle. *Damn!*

'Finally, I'd want you to take your evening meal in the dining room with me.'

So she could keep an eye on him—assess his mental state. He could feel his nostrils flare as he dragged in a breath. He was tempted to tell her to go to hell, except...

Except he might have given up caring about him-self, but he hadn't given up caring about Russ. His brother might be eleven and a half years older than Mac, but they'd always been close. Russ had al-ways looked out for him. The least Mac could do now was look out for Russ in whatever limited capacity he could. With Russ's health so tenuous Mac couldn't risk adding to his stress levels.

Jo's phone rang. She pulled it from the back pocket of her jeans. He stared at that hip and something stirred inside him. And then desire hit him— hot and hard. He blinked. He turned away to hide the evidence, adjusting his jeans as he pretended an interest in the horizon.

What on earth…? He liked his women slim and compact, polished and poised. Jo Anderson might be poised, but as for the rest of it…

He dragged a hand back through his hair. There was no denying, though, that his body reacted to her like a bee to honey. He swallowed. It was probably to be expected, right? He'd been cooped up here away from all human contact for four months. This was just a natural male reaction to the female form.

'I don't know, Russ.'

That snapped him back.

'Yeah…' She flicked a glance in his direction. 'I've seen him.'

Mac winced at her tone.

'You have yourself a deal.' He pitched his words low, so they wouldn't carry down the phone to Russ, but they still came out savage. He couldn't help it. He held up one finger. 'Give me one week.'

'Hmm… Well, he's looking a little peaky—as if he's had the flu or a tummy bug.'

He seized her free hand. Startled sage eyes met his. 'Please,' he whispered.

The softness and warmth of her hand seeped into him and almost made him groan, and then her hand tightened about his and his mouth went dry in a millisecond.

When she shook herself free of him a moment later he let out a breath he hadn't even realised he'd been holding.

'I expect it's nothing that a bit of rest, gentle exercise, home-cooked food and sun won't put to rights in a week or two.'

He closed his eyes and gave thanks.

'Nah, I promise. I won't take any risks. I'll call a doctor in if he hasn't picked up in a few days. Here—you want to talk to him?'

And before Mac could shake his head and back away he found the phone thrust out to him.

He swallowed the bile that rose in his throat and took it. 'Hey, Russ, how you doing?'

'Better than you, by the sounds of it. Though it explains why you haven't answered my last two calls.'

He winced. 'It's all I've been able to do to keep

up with my email.' *I'm sorry, bro.* He hadn't been good for anyone. Least of all his brother.

'Well, you listen to Jo, okay? She's got a good head on her shoulders.'

He glanced at said head and noticed how the wavy dark hair gleamed in the sun, and how cute little freckles sprinkled a path across the bridge of her nose. She had a rather cute nose. She cocked an eyebrow and he cleared his throat.

'Will do,' he forced himself to say.

'Good. I want you in the best of health when I come to visit.'

He choked back a cough. Russ was coming to visit?

'Give my love to Jo.'

With that, Russ hung up. Mac stared at Jo. 'When is he coming to visit?'

She shrugged and plucked her phone from his fingers.

'Why is he coming?'

'Oh, that one's easy. Because he loves you. He wants to see you before he goes under the knife.' She met his gaze. 'In case he doesn't wake up after the operation.'

'That's crazy.'

'Is it?'

'Russ is going to be just fine!' His brother didn't need to exert himself in any fashion until he was a hundred per cent fit again.

She stared at him for a long moment. 'Are you familiar with the Banjo Paterson poem "The Man From Snowy River"?'

Her question threw him. 'Sure.'

'Can you remember what comes after the first couple of lines? "There was movement at the station, for the word had passed around that the colt from old Regret had got away…".'

'"And had joined the wild bush horses—he was worth a thousand pound, So all the cracks had gathered to the fray",' he recited. His class had memorised that in the third grade.

'Wild… Worth… Fray…' she murmured in that honeyed liquid sunshine voice of hers.

'Why?'

She shook herself. 'No reason. Just an earworm.'

She seized her suitcases and strode back towards the house with them, and he couldn't help feeling his fate had just been sealed by a poem.

And then it hit him.

Honey! The ingredient he'd been searching for was honey.

CHAPTER TWO

Jo took a couple of deep breaths before spooning spaghetti and meatballs onto two plates. If Mac said something cutting about her efforts in the kitchen she'd—

She'd dump the contents of his plate in his lap?

She let out a slow breath. It was a nice fantasy, but she wouldn't. She'd just act calm and unconcerned, as she always did, and pretend the slings and arrows didn't touch her.

Seizing the plates, she strode into the dining room. She set one in front of Mac and the other at her place opposite. He didn't so much as glance at the food, but he did glare at her. Was he going to spend the entire week sulking?

What fun.

She stared back, refusing to let him cow her. She'd expected the shouting and the outrage. After all, he wasn't known as 'Mad Mac'—television's most notorious and demanding celebrity chef— for nothing. The tabloids had gone to town on him after the accident, claiming it would never have happened if 'Mad Mac' hadn't been so intimidating.

She bit back a sigh. It was all nonsense, of course. She'd had the inside scoop on Mac from Russ. She knew all of that onscreen TV shouting had been a front—a ploy to send the ratings skyrocketing. It had worked too. So it hadn't surprised her that he'd donned that persona when she'd stormed in on him earlier. But the sulking threw her.

'What?' he bit out when she continued to stare.

She shook herself. 'For what we are about to receive, may the Lord make us truly thankful. Amen.' She picked up her cutlery and sliced into a meatball.

'You're religious?'

'No.' The prayer had just seemed a convenient way to handle an awkward silence. 'I mean, I do believe in something bigger than us—whatever that may be.'

Mac didn't say anything. He didn't even move to pick up his cutlery.

She forged on. 'One of the guys on the mineral exploration camps was a Christian and we all got into the habit of saying Grace. It's nice. It doesn't hurt to remember the things we should be grateful for.'

His frown deepened to a scowl. 'You really think that's going to work? You really think you can make my life seem okay just by—?'

She slammed her knife and fork down. 'Not everything is about you, Mac.' She forced her eyes wide. 'Some of it might even be about me.' Couldn't he at least look at his food? He needn't think it would taste any better cold. 'Your attitude sucks. You know that? Frankly, I don't care if you've decided to self-destruct or not, but you can darn well wait until after Russ has recovered from his bypass surgery to do it.'

'You're not exactly polite company, are you?'

'Neither are you. Besides, I refuse to put any effort into being good company for as long as you sulk. I'm not your mother. It's not my job to cajole you into a better temper.'

His jaw dropped.

And he still hadn't touched his food.

'Eat something, Mac. If we're busy eating we can abandon any pretence at small talk.'

A laugh choked out of him and just for a moment it transformed him. Oh, the burn scars on the left side of his face and neck were still as angry and livid as ever, but his mouth hooked up and his eyes momentarily brightened and he held his head at an angle she remembered from his television show.

It was why she was still here. Earlier this afternoon he'd fired up—not with humour, but with intensity and passion. He'd become the man she'd recognised from the TV, but also from Russ's descriptions. *That* was a man she could work with.

Finally he did as she bade and forked a small mouthful of meatball and sauce into his mouth. When he didn't gag, a knot of tension eased out of her.

'This isn't bad.' He ate some more and frowned. 'In fact, it's pretty good.'

Yeah, right. He was just trying to butter her up, frightened of what she might tell Russ.

'Actually, it's very good—considering the state of the pantry.'

She almost believed him. Almost. 'I'll need to shop for groceries tomorrow. I understand we're halfway between Forster and Taree here. Any suggestions for where I should go?'

'No.'

When he didn't add anything she shook her head and set to eating. It had been a long day and she was tired and hungry. She halted with half a meatball practically in her mouth when she realised he'd stopped eating and was staring at her.

'What?'

'I wasn't being rude. It's just that I haven't been to either town. I was getting groceries delivered from a supermarket in Forster.'

'Was?'

He scowled. 'The delivery man couldn't follow instructions.'

Ah. Said delivery man had probably encroached on Mac's precious privacy. 'Right. Well, I'll try my luck in Forster, then.' She'd seen signposts for the town before turning off to Mac's property.

He got back to work on the plate in front of him with... She blinked. With *gusto*? Heat spread through her stomach. *Oh, don't be ridiculous!* He'd had his own TV show. He was a consummate actor. But the heat didn't dissipate.

She pulled in a breath. 'I'm hoping Russ warned you that I'm not much of a cook.'

He froze. Very slowly he lowered his cutlery. 'Russ said you were a good plain cook. On this evening's evidence I'd agree with him.' His face turned opaque. 'You're feeling intimidated cooking for a...?'

'World-renowned chef?' she finished for him.

'Yes, a little. I just want you to keep your expectations within that realm of plain, please.'

She bit back a sigh. Plain—what a boring word. *Beauty is as beauty does.* The old adage sounded through her mind. *Yeah, yeah, whatever.*

'I promise not to criticise your cooking. I will simply be…' he grimaced '…grateful for whatever you serve up. You don't need to worry that I'll be secretly judging your technique.'

'I expect there'd be nothing secret about it. I think you'd be more than happy to share your opinions on the matter.'

His lips twitched.

'Is there anything you don't eat?' she rushed on, not wanting to dwell on those lips for too long.

He shook his head.

'Is there anything in particular you'd like me to serve?'

He shook his head again.

There was something else she'd meant to ask him… *Oh, that's right.* 'You have a garage…'

They both reached for the plate of garlic bread at the same time. He waited for her to take a slice first. He had nice hands. She remembered admiring them when she'd watched him on TV. Lean, long-fingered hands that looked strong and—

'The garage?'

She shook herself. 'Would there be room for me to park my car in there? I expect this sea air is pretty tough on a car's bodywork.'

'Feel free.'

'Thank you.'

They both crunched garlic bread. He watched her from the corner of his eye. She chewed and swallowed, wondering what he made of her. She sure as heck wasn't like the women he was forever being photographed with in the papers. For starters she was as tall as a lot of men, and more athletic than most.

Not Mac, though. Even in his current out-of-form condition he was still taller and broader than her—though she might give him a run for his money in an arm wrestle at the moment.

Her stomach tightened. He was probably wondering what god he'd cheesed off to have a woman like *her* landing on his doorstep. Mac was a golden boy. Beautiful. And she was the opposite. Not that *that* had anything to do with anything. What he thought of her physically made no difference whatsoever.

Except, of course, it did. It always mattered.

'You've shown a lot of concern for Russ.'

Her head came up. 'Yes?'

He scowled at her. 'Are you in love with him? He's too old for you, you know.'

It surprised her so much she laughed. 'You're kidding, right?' She swept her garlic bread through the leftover sauce on her plate.

His frown deepened. 'No.'

'I love your brother as a friend, but I'm not in love with him. Lord, what a nightmare *that* would be.' She sat back and wiped her fingers on a serviette.

'Why?'

'I'm not a masochist. You and your brother have similar tastes in women. You both date petite, perfectly made-up blondes who wear killer heels and flirty dresses.' She hadn't packed a dress. She didn't even own a pair of heels.

He pushed his plate away, his face darkening. 'How the hell do *you* know what type I like?' He turned sideways in his chair to cross his legs. It hid his scarring from her view.

'It's true I'm basing my assumption on who you've been snapped with in the tabloids and what Russ has told me.'

'You make us sound shallow.'

If the shoe fits...

'But I can assure you that the women you just described wouldn't look twice at me now.'

'Only if they were superficial.'

His head jerked up.

'And beauty and superficiality don't necessarily go hand in hand.'

No more than plain and stupid, or plain and thick-skinned.

He opened his mouth, but she continued on over the top of him. 'Anyway, you're not going to get any sympathy from me on that. I've never been what people consider beautiful. I've learned to value other things. You think people will no longer find you beautiful—

'I *know* they won't!'

He was wrong, but... 'So welcome to the club.'

His jaw dropped.

'It's not the end of the world, you know?'

He stared at her for a long moment and then leaned across the table. 'What the hell are you *really* doing here, Jo Anderson?'

She stared back at him, and inside she started to weep—because she wanted to ask this man to teach her to cook and he was so damaged and angry that she knew he would toss her request on the rubbish heap and not give it so much as the time of day.

Something in his eyes gentled. 'Jo?'

Now wasn't the time to raise the subject. It was becoming abundantly clear that there might never be a good time.

She waved a hand in the air. 'The answer is two-fold.' It wasn't a lie. 'I'm here to make sure you don't undo all the hard work I've put into Russ.'

He sat back. 'Hard work?'

She should rise and clear away their plates, clean the kitchen, but he deserved some answers. 'Do you know how hard, how physically demanding, it is to perform CPR for five straight minutes?' Which was what she'd done for Russ.

He shook his head, his eyes darkening.

'It's really hard. And all the while your mind is screaming in panic and making deals with the universe.'

'Deals?'

'Please let Russ live and I'll never say another mean word about anyone ever again. Please let Russ live and I promise to be a better granddaughter and great-niece. Please let Russ live and I'll do whatever you ask, will face my worst fears… Blah, blah, blah.' She pushed her hair back off her face.

'You know—the usual promises that are nearly impossible to keep.' She stared down at her glass of water. 'It was the longest five minutes of my life.'

'But Russ did live. You did save his life. It's an extraordinary thing.'

'Yes.'

'And now you want to make sure that I don't harm his recovery?'

'Something like that.'

'Which is why you're here—to check up on me so you can ease Russ's mind?'

'He was going to come himself, and that didn't seem wise.'

Mac turned grey.

'But you don't have it quite right. Russ is doing me a favour, organising this job for me.'

He remained silent, not pressing her, and she was grateful for that.

'You see, Russ's heart attack and my fear that he was going to die brought me face to face with my own mortality.'

He flinched and she bit back a curse. What did she know about mortality compared to this man? She reached across to clasp his hand in a sign of automatic sympathy, but he froze. A bad taste rose in her mouth and she pulled her hand back into her lap. Her heart pounded. He wouldn't welcome her touch. Of course he wouldn't.

'I expect you know what I'm talking about.'

Mac's accident had left him with serious burns, but it had left a young apprentice fighting for his life. She remembered Russ's relief when the young man had finally been taken off the critical list.

'What I'm trying to say is that it's made me reassess my life. It's forced me to admit I wasn't very happy, that I didn't really like my job. I don't want to spend the next twenty years feeling like that.'

She blew out a breath.

'So when Russ found out you needed a house-keeper and mentioned it to me I jumped at the chance. It'll give me two or three months to come up with a game plan.'

Mac stared at her. 'You're changing careers?'

'Uh-huh.' She looked a bit green.

'To do what?'

She turned greener. 'I have absolutely no idea.'

He knew that feeling.

Mac didn't want to be touched by her story—he didn't want to be touched by anything—but he was. Maybe it was the sheer simplicity of the telling, the lack of fanfare. Or maybe it was because he understood that sense of dissatisfaction she described. He'd stalled out here in his isolation and his self-pity while she was determined to surge forward.

Maybe if he watched her he'd learn—

He cut that thought off. He didn't deserve the chance to move forward. He'd ruined a man's life. He deserved to spend the rest of his life making amends.

But not at the expense of other people. Like Russ. Or Jo.

'You're wrong, you know?'

She glanced up. 'About…?'

'You seem to think you're plain—invisible, even.' *Not beautiful.*

'Invisible?' She snorted. 'I'm six feet tall with a build some charitably call generous. Invisible is the one thing I'm not.'

'Generous' was the perfect word to describe her. She had glorious curves in all the right places. A fact that his male hormones acknowledged and appreciated even while his brain told him to leave that well enough alone.

He leaned back, careful to keep the good side of his face to her. 'You're a very striking woman.' *Don't drool.* 'So what if you're tall? You're in proportion.' She looked strong, athletic and full of life. 'You have lovely eyes, your hair is shiny, and you have skin that most women would kill for. You may not fit in with conventional magazine cover ideals of beauty, but it doesn't mean you aren't beautiful. Stop selling yourself short. I can assure you that you're not plain.'

She gaped at him. It made him scowl and shuffle back in his seat. 'Well, you're not.'

She snapped her mouth shut. She wiped her hands down the front of her shirt, which only proved to him how truly womanly she happened to be. The colour in her cheeks deepened as if she'd read that thought in his face.

'There's another reason I'm here,' she blurted out.

The hurried confession and the way her words tripped over themselves, the fact that she looked cute when flustered, all conspired to make him want to grin. He couldn't remember the last time he'd smiled, let alone grinned. He resisted the urge now too. In the end, grinning… Well, it would just make things harder, in the same way the sunlight and the sea breeze did.

But he did take pity on her. 'Another reason?' he prompted.

She moistened her lips. Like the rest of her they were generous, and full of promise.

'Mac, one of the reasons I came out here was to ask if you would teach me to cook.' She grimaced. 'Well, if we're being completely accurate, if you'd teach me to make a *macaron* tower.'

His every muscle froze. His nerve-endings started to scream. For a moment all he could see in his mind was fire—all red and heat. A lump the size of a saucepan wedged in his throat. It took three goes to swallow it.

'No.' The word croaked out of him.

He closed his eyes to force air into protesting lungs and then opened them again, his skin growing slick with perspiration.

'No.' The single word came out cold and clear. 'That's out of the question. I don't cook any more.'

'But—'

'Ever.' He pinned her with his gaze and knew it must be pitiless when she shivered. 'It's absolutely out of the question.'

He rose.

'Now if you don't mind. I'm going to do a bit of work before I retire for the night. I'll move my sleeping quarters to the end bedroom tomorrow.'

She seemed to gather herself. 'I'll clean it first thing.'

That reminded him that she meant to do a grocery shop tomorrow too. 'There's housekeeping money in the tin on the mantel in the kitchen.'

'Right.'

He hated the way she surveyed him. Turning his back, he left, forcing knees that trembled to carry him up the stairs and into his room. He lowered himself to the chair at his desk and dropped his head to his hands, did what he could to quieten the scream stretching through his brain.

Teach Jo to cook?

Impossible.

His chest pounded in time with his temples. Blood surged in his ears, deafening him. He didn't know how long it took for the pounding to slow, for his chest to unclench, and for his breathing to regain a more natural rhythm. It felt like a lifetime.

Eventually he lifted his head. He couldn't teach her to cook. She'd saved his brother's life and he owed her, but he couldn't teach her to cook.

He rose and went to the double glass doors. With the curtains pushed back they stood open to the moonlight. Below, starlight dappled navy water.

He couldn't teach her to cook, but he could do everything else she'd asked of him. He could ensure that Russ didn't have one thing to worry about on Mac's account.

One week of halfway human behaviour? He could manage that.

He thought back to the way he'd just left the dining room and dragged a hand through his hair. She must think him a madman. Hauling in a breath, he rested his forehead against cool glass. He might not be able to help her on the cooking front, but could he help her in her search for a new vocation?

The sooner she found a new direction the sooner she'd go, leaving him in peace again. A low, savage laugh scraped from his throat. He would never find peace. He didn't deserve it. But he could have her gone. He'd settle for that.

Mac had been awake for over an hour before he heard Jo's firm tread on the stairs. She moved past his door and on to the bedroom at the end. No doubt to clean it, as she'd promised. The need for caffeine pounded through him. So far he'd resisted it—not ready to face Jo yet.

He blamed the light pouring in at the windows. It had disorientated him.

Liar. It wasn't the light but a particular woman he found disorientating.

He could bolt down to the kitchen now, while she was busy up here.

Yeah, like *that* would convince her to tell Russ all was fine and dandy. He flung the covers back, pulled on a clean pair of jeans and a sweater, and stomped into the en-suite bathroom to splash water on his face. He stood by his bedroom door, counted to three, dragging in a breath on each count before opening it.

'Morning, Jo,' he called out. Amazingly his voice didn't emerge all hoarse and croaky as he'd expected.

She appeared at the end of the hallway. 'Good morning. Sleep well?'

Surprisingly, he had. 'Yeah, thanks.' He remembered his manners. 'And you?'

'No.'

She didn't add any further explanation. He took a step towards her, careful to keep the right side of his face to her. With all the curtains on this level now open there was a lot of light to contend with.

'Is there something wrong with your room? The bed? The mattress?'

She laughed and something inside him unhitched. 'I never sleep well in a new place the first night. Plus, I did a lot of driving yesterday and that always makes me feel unsettled. I'll sleep like a dream tonight.'

He rolled his shoulders. 'How long did you drive for?'

'Five hours.'

Five hours? And she'd arrived to... His stomach churned. She'd arrived to his bitterness, resentment and utter rudeness.

'Mac, we need to talk about my duties.'

That snapped him to.

'I mean, do you want me to make you a full cooked breakfast each morning? What about lunch?'

He noticed she didn't give him any quarter as far as dinner went. 'I'll help myself for breakfast and lunch.'

'Not a breakfast person, huh?'

He wasn't. He opened his mouth. He closed it again and waited for a lecture.

'Me neither,' she confessed. 'Most important meal of the day, blah, blah, blah.' She rolled her eyes. 'Just give me a coffee before I kill you.'

He laughed, but he was still careful to keep his good side to her. She hadn't flinched at his scars last night or so far this morning. But he knew what they looked like. He could at least spare her when he could.

One thing was for sure—she didn't treat him like an invalid, and he was grateful for it.

'There's a pot of freshly brewed coffee on the hob.'

He didn't need any further encouragement, and turned in the direction of the kitchen.

He swung back before he reached the stairs. 'Jo?'

Her head appeared in the bedroom doorway again.

'Don't bust a gut trying to get the house ship-shape all at once, will you?' He'd long since dismissed his army of hired help. 'I've…uh…let it get away from me a bit.' At her raised eyebrow he amended that to 'A lot.'

She merely saluted him and went back to work. He made his way down to the kitchen, wondering if he'd passed the *don't worry Russ* test so far this morning. He poured himself a coffee, took a sip and closed his eyes. Man, the woman could make a fine brew.

Mac clocked the exact moment Jo returned from her shopping expedition.

His first instinct was to continue hiding out in

his room. He stared at the half-written recipe on his computer screen and pushed to his feet. If he walked away and did something else for half an hour he might remember if he reduced the recipe's required infusion by a third or a quarter.

If he could just see it in the saucepan and smell it he'd have the answer in an instant and—

He cut the thought off with a curse and went to help Jo unpack the car. She'd only given him a week. He'd better make the most of it.

She glanced up when he strode out onto the veranda, and in the light of her grace and vigour he suddenly felt awkward and ungainly.

He scowled, unable to dredge up a single piece of small talk. 'I thought I'd help unpack the car.'

She pursed her lips and he realised he was still scowling. He did what he could to smooth his face out — the parts of his face he *could* smooth out.

'You have any trouble finding the shops?'

Heck. Scintillating conversation.

'None at all. You feeling okay, Mac?'

'I'm fine.' Striding to the car, he seized as many bags as he could and stalked back into the house with them.

It took them two trips.

He wasn't quite sure what to do after that, so

he leant against the sink and pretended to drink a glass of water as he watched her unpack the groceries. There were the expected trays of meat—hamburger mince, sausages, steak and diced beef. And then there was the unexpected and to be deplored—frozen pies and frozen pizza. Fish fingers, for heaven's sake!

He flicked a disparaging finger at the boxes. What are those?'

'I'm assuming you're not asking the question literally?'

She'd donned one of those mock patient voices used on troublesome children and it set his teeth on edge. 'Is this to punish me for refusing to teach you to cook?'

She turned from stowing stuff in the freezer, hands on hips. 'You told me you weren't a fussy eater.'

'This isn't *food*. It's processed pap!'

'You're free to refuse to eat anything I serve up.'

'But if I do you'll go running to Russ to tell tales?'

She grinned, and her relish both irked and amused him.

She lifted one hand. 'Rock.' She lifted the other. 'Hard place.'

Which described his situation perfectly.

She grinned again and his mouth watered. She seized a packet of frozen pies and waved them at him. 'Pies, mash, peas and gravy is one of my all-time favourite, walk-over-hot-coals-to-get-it meals, and I'm not giving it up—not even for your high-falutin' standards. And before you ask—no, I haven't mastered the trick to pastry.' She shook her head. 'Life's too short to fuss with pastry. Or to stuff a mushroom.'

She was wrong. A perfect buttery pastry, light and delicate, was one of life's adventures. And mushroom-stuffing shouldn't be sneezed at. But why on earth would she ask him to teach her to cook if that was the way she felt?

'And I'll have you know that fish fingers on a fresh bun with a dollop of tartare sauce makes the best lunch.'

'I will *never* eat fish fingers.'

'All the more for me, then.'

He scowled at the pizza boxes.

'Also,' her lips twitched, 'as far as I'm concerned, there's no such thing as a bad slice of pizza.'

'That's ludicrous!'

'Don't be such a snob. Besides, all of this food is better than whatever it is you've been living on for the last heaven only knows how long. Which, as far as I can tell, has been tinned baked beans, crackers and breakfast cereal.'

She had a point. It didn't matter what he ate. In fact the more cardboard-like and tasteless the better. It had been his search for excellence and his ambition that had caused the fire that had almost claimed a young man's life and—

His chest cramped. He reached out an unsteady hand and lowered himself into a chair at the table. He had to remember what was important. He wanted to do all he could to set Russ's mind at rest, but he couldn't lose sight of what was important—and that was paying off his debts.

A warm hand on his shoulder brought him back to himself. 'Mac, are you okay?'

He nodded.

'Don't lie to me. Do you need a doctor?'

'No.'

'Russell told me you were physically recovered.'

'I am.' He pulled in a breath. 'It's just that I don't like talking about food or cooking.'

Realisation dawned in those sage-green eyes of hers. 'Because it reminds you of the accident?'

It reminded him of all he'd had. And all he'd lost.

CHAPTER THREE

MAC TENSED BENEATH her touch and Jo snatched her hand back, suddenly and searingly aware that while Mac wasn't in peak physical condition he was still a man. He still had broader shoulders than most men she knew, and beneath the thin cotton of his sweater his body pulsed hot and vibrant.

But at this moment he looked so bowed and defeated she wanted to wrap her arms around him and tell him it would all be okay, that it would work itself out.

She grimaced. She could just imagine the way he'd flinch from her if she did. Besides, she didn't know if it *would* be all right. She didn't know if it would work itself out or not.

She moved away to the other side of the kitchen. 'I can make you one promise, Mac.'

He glanced up.

'I promise to never feed you fish fingers.'

He didn't laugh. He didn't even smile. But something inside him unhitched a fraction and his colour started to return. 'I suppose I should give thanks for small mercies.'

'Absolutely. Have you had lunch yet?'

He shook his head.

She seized an apple from the newly replenished fruit bowl and tossed it to him.

This time she'd have sworn he'd laugh, but he didn't.

'I can see I'm going to get nothing but the very best care while you're here.'

'Top-notch,' she agreed. She grabbed her car keys from the bench. 'I'm going to put The Beast in the garage.'

Mac didn't say anything. He just bit into his apple.

The moment she was out of sight Jo's shoulders sagged. If Mac looked like that—so sick and grey and full of despair—just at the thought of the accident, at the thought of cooking...

She had no hope of getting him to give her cooking lessons. None at all. She twisted her fingers together. It was obvious now that it had been insensitive and unkind to have asked.

Why do you never think, Jo?

With a sigh, she started up her car and drove it around to the garage. It didn't solve her problem.

She needed to make a *macaron* tower and she had just over two months to learn how to do it.

She pushed her shoulders back. Fine. She had a whole two months. She'd just teach herself. There'd be recipes online, and videos. What else was she going to do out here? Keeping house and cooking dinner would take—what?—three or four hours a day tops? Probably less once she had the house in order.

A *macaron* tower? How hard could it be?

'Don't say that,' she murmured, leaping out of her car to lift the roller door to one of the garage's two bays. The bay she'd chosen stood empty. Out of curiosity she lifted the second door too.

She had a French cookbook Great-Aunt Edith had given her. Maybe there was something in there—

Her thoughts slammed to a halt. She stood there, hands still attached to the roller door, and gaped at the vision of loveliness that had appeared in front of her.

Eventually she lowered her hands, wiped them down the sides of her jeans. Oh. My. Word.

Oh.
Dear.
Lord.

The sky-blue classic eighties sports car was her very own fantasy car brought to life and it was all she could do to not drop to her knees and kiss it.

'Oh, my God, you are the most beautiful car ever,' she whispered, daring to trail a finger across the bodywork as she completed a full circle around it, admiring the front curves, the fat spoiler, its gloss, its clean lines and its shape. What wouldn't she do to test drive this car?

What wouldn't she do just to sit in one!

She tried the driver's door. Locked.

With a jump, she spun around and closed the garage door. One needed to protect a piece of perfection like this from damaging elements. She parked The Beast in the bay beside the sleek machine.

Beauty and The Beast.

She cast one more longing look at Mac's beautiful car before closing the second roller door and racing into the house. Mac was still in the kitchen—eating a sandwich now, rather than the apple.

He glanced up when she clattered in. 'I take it I'm allowed to help myself to the provisions?'

'You have my dream car in your garage!'

'Is that a yes?'

How could he be so cool? She gaped at him and

then mentally kicked herself. She spread her arms wide. 'Of course! You can help yourself to anything.'

He stared at her and his eyes darkened. He licked his lips and she had a sudden feeling he wasn't thinking about food, but an altogether different primal need. She pulled her arms back to her sides, heat flooding her veins. *Don't be ridiculous.* Men like Mac didn't find women like her attractive.

Mac turned away from her on his chair as if he'd just come to the same conclusion. She dragged a hand back through her hair to rub her nape.

'You said something about my car?'

She swallowed back the request that he let her drive it—just once. She swallowed back asking him if he'd just let her sit in it. For all she knew that might be as insensitive as asking him to teach her to cook.

'I… It's beautiful.'

He glanced at her, raised an eyebrow, and she shrugged, unsure what to say, unsure what constituted a safe topic—because she never wanted to witness that look of defeat and despair on his face again. So she shrugged again and filled the jug. She measured out tea leaves.

'Feel free to take it for a spin any time you want.'

The jug wobbled precariously as she poured boiling water into the teapot.

Mac leapt up. 'Don't burn yourself!'

She concentrated on setting the jug back in its place. 'I didn't spill a drop.' Her heart thump-thumped. 'I'm fine.' She set the teapot and two mugs onto the table. 'But I gotta tell you, Mac, you shouldn't offer a girl her heart's desire while she's pouring out boiling water—and for future reference probably not while she's wielding sharp implements either.'

She smiled as she said it. Mac didn't smile back. He just stared at the jug with haunted eyes, the pulse in his throat pounding.

She sat down as if nothing in the world was amiss. 'Would you truly let me take your car out for a drive?'

He sat too. He wiped a hand down his face before lifting one negligent shoulder. 'Sure.' But he reached out to pour the tea before she could. 'It could use a run. I turn it over a couple of times a week, but I don't take it out.'

She gaped at him. 'You'd let me drive it? Just like that?'

That same slow lift of his shoulder. 'Why not?'

It took an effort of will to drag her gaze from

that broad sweep of corded muscle. 'I…uh… What if I pranged it?'

'The insurance would cover it. Jo, it's just a car.'

'No, it's not. It's…' She reached out to try and pluck the appropriate description from the air. 'It's a gem, a jewel—a thing of beauty. It's—'

'Just a car.'

'A piece of precision German engineering.'

She almost asked how he could not want to drive it, but choked the question back at the last moment. That *would* be tactless. He'd been in the most dreadful accident, had suffered a long and painful recovery, and would bear the scars for the rest of his life. He'd been hounded by the media. She could see how fast cars might have lost their appeal.

So why hadn't he sold it?

She stared at him and pursed her lips. Maybe Mac hadn't given up on life as completely as he thought.

He glared. 'What?'

'You wouldn't consider selling it, would you?'

He blinked. 'Could you afford it?'

'I've been working in the Outback for the last eight years, making decent money but having very little to spend it on.'

He scratched a hand through his hair. 'But you're not earning a decent wage now.'

She was earning enough to cover her needs.

He jabbed a finger at her. 'And you may, in fact, be training for a new job shortly.'

'I suppose it wouldn't be the most practical of moves.'

He glared. 'You can say that again.'

He didn't want to sell it! She bit back a grin. There was still some life in Mac after all.

He settled back in his seat with a *harrumph*. 'But the offer stands. You can take it for a spin any time you want.'

'Lord, don't say that,' she groaned, 'or your house will never get cleaned.'

He laughed. It made his eyes dance, it softened his lips, and Jo couldn't drag her gaze away. 'You… uh…' She moistened her lips. 'You wouldn't want to come along for a spin?'

His face was immediately shuttered, closed, and she could have kicked herself. 'Well, no, I guess not. You're busy writing up your recipes and stuff.'

'Speaking of which…' He rose, evidently intent on getting back to work.

She surveyed his retreating back with a sinking heart. *Well done, Jo.*

In the next moment he returned. He poured himself a second cup of tea before unhitching a set of keys from the wall and setting them in front of her. 'Ms Anderson, you brew a mighty fine pot of coffee and not a bad cup of tea. Reward yourself and take the car for a spin.'

She shook her head. 'Not until I have your house looking spotless.' It would be a nice treat to spur her on. 'Maybe the day after tomorrow.'

He merely shrugged and left the keys on the table.

After lunch, two days later, Jo made a pot of tea and poured a mug for both her and Mac. Mac reached across to rattle the keys to his car. For the last two days those keys had sat on the table, where they'd tempted, teased and cajoled Jo mercilessly. Neither she nor Mac had put them back on the hook

'Does the house pass muster?' he asked.

Yes, it did. And so did the driveway since she'd found a pile of blue metal gravel out behind the garage. She'd used it to fill in the worst of the potholes along the driveway.

'You can retract your offer any time,' she told him.

'I'm not going to retract the offer, Jo. Go take the car for a spin and enjoy yourself.'

He tossed her the keys. She stared down at them, and then at him. 'I won't be gone long—maybe twenty or thirty minutes tops.'

He shrugged as if he didn't care how long she'd be gone. 'Just don't get a speeding ticket,' he tossed over his shoulder, before taking his mug and heading back upstairs to his mysterious work.

She wondered how on earth he could write recipes if he didn't cook them first.

She wondered how he could bear not to take his beautiful car out for a drive.

She drained her tea and then headed straight out to the garage. Would she even fit into the low-slung sports car? She planted her hands on her hips. If Mac did then she would too. She folded herself into it and sat for a long time, revelling in the moment and familiarising herself with the dashboard, the gears, the fact the indicator was on the left of the steering wheel rather than the right.

She started it up and gave a purr of delight at the throaty sound of the turbo engine. Would the reality of driving this car live up to the fantasy?

She negotiated the driveway with ludicrous care. She had no intention of bringing this car back in anything but perfect condition. When she finally reached the open road she let out a yell of pure delight, relishing the perfect handling, the smooth ride and the responsive power of the car. A body could get addicted to the sheer exhilaration!

After her first initial experimentation with the accelerator she made sure to stick to the speed limit. Instead of speed she savoured the way the car handled the twists and turns of these old country roads.

Oh, how could Mac stand to leave this amazing car in his garage and not use it?

She explored the roads that branched off from Mac's property, along with a couple of others that it seemed justifiable to explore, and discovered two tiny hamlets—Diamond Beach and Hallidays Point—both of which had tiny general stores if she needed to pop out for bread or milk. She also discovered more glorious coastal scenery.

Mac had certainly chosen a beautiful part of the world for his exile. Odd, then, that he didn't seem to spend much time appreciating it, that he'd taken such pains to shut it out from his sight.

It was grief, she supposed. Grief at having lost the life he'd had. There was no denying that until six months ago it had been a charmed life. Maybe when his grief had had time to abate he'd see a way forward again. Perhaps he'd realise his old life wasn't irrevocably lost to him forever.

Not if he refuses to cook.

She sighed, but a signpost pointing down another winding road had her slowing. *'Dog Shelter'*. A grin built through her and on impulse she turned down the road.

Mac will freak!

So what?

It's his house.

Nothing had been said about not being allowed a pet.

She turned into the signposted driveway. She wasn't the only person at the dog shelter. An elderly man emerged from the back of a small sedan as she pulled up beside it. A border collie leapt out behind him.

A woman dressed in overalls strode up from a nearby dog run. 'Mr Cole? And I expect this is Bandit?' She nodded to tell Jo she'd be with her shortly.

Mr Cole's hand dropped to Bandit's head and tears filled his eyes. 'It breaks my heart to leave him.'

Jo's throat thickened.

The woman glanced at the younger couple who had remained in the car. 'Your family can't take him?'

He shook his head and Jo had a feeling that *won't* rather than 'can't' was the operative word on that.

'Please find a good home for him. He's such a good boy and has been such a good pal. If I wasn't going into a nursing home I'd…'

Jo couldn't stand it any more. She leapt forward. 'Oh, please let me take him. He's beautiful and I promise to love him.'

And then she was on her knees in front of Bandit, who obligingly licked her face. As she ran her hands through his fur she realised what a spectacle she must look. She rose, aware of how much she towered over Mr Cole and Bandit—not to mention the dog shelter lady.

'I was driving past and saw the sign and…well, it suddenly occurred to me that I'm at a point in my life where I can offer a dog a good home.'

Did that make her sound like a stark raving lunatic? Or a responsible, prospective dog owner?

'Maybe…' She swallowed. 'Maybe, Mr Cole, I could bring Bandit to visit you in your new home?'

* * *

Mac paced back and forth along the veranda. Jo had been gone for over an hour.

An hour!

Anything could have happened to her. His stomach churned. She could be lying in a ditch somewhere. Or wrapped around a tree. What had he been thinking to let her go driving off like that on her own? Had she even driven a performance car before? Why hadn't he gone with her?

He closed his eyes. He'd have enjoyed it too much. His hands fisted. If he didn't keep fighting the distractions this cookbook would never get written.

And he had to finish it.

He gripped the railing and stared out to sea. Jo was capable. She'd be fine. He drew air into his lungs. Of course she'd be fine. She'd just be caught up in the experience.

He knew exactly what that felt like.

He started pacing again. He hadn't done any real maintenance on the car since he'd buried himself out here. What if it had broken down? What if she was stuck on the side of the road somewhere? Did she have her phone with her?

He dug out his own phone to check for messages.

Nothing.

At that exact moment he heard the low rumble of the car's engine and he had to lower himself to the top step as relief punched through him. He closed his eyes and gave thanks. Jo was his responsibility, and—

Since when?

She was an employee, and that made her his responsibility.

Responsibility *and* a thorn in his side.

Nonetheless, when she parked the car in front of the house it took all his strength to remain where he was rather than leap down the stairs, haul her from the car and hug her. Those would be the actions of a crazy man. And, despite her first impressions of him, Mac wasn't crazy.

She bounced out of the car with a grin that held a hint of trepidation and, thorn in his side or not, he silently acknowledged how glad he was to see her.

'Have fun?' he managed.

'I didn't mean to be gone so long. I hope I didn't worry you?' She sent him a wary glance. 'The car is amazing.'

He tried to tamp down on the rising wave of enthusiasm he felt for the car too. 'I'm glad it lived up to expectations.'

'Oh, it exceeded them.'

He closed his eyes and refused to ask her how she'd felt as she'd swept around a wide bend in the road, or what she thought of the vehicle's magnificent acceleration.

'But I got a bit distracted.'

He snapped his eyes open and leapt to his feet. Had she scratched his car?

'What do you mean—?'

And he found a dog sitting at her feet. His jaw dropped.

'You put a *dog* in my car?'

'I… We made sure to use a blanket so Bandit, here, wouldn't damage the upholstery.'

He stared at her. 'You put a flea-ridden mutt in my car?'

She grimaced, shifting from one foot to the other.

Get over it, pal, he told himself.

Get over it? That car was his most treasured possession! It—

He suddenly flashed to Ethan, in the burns unit at the hospital, and had to lower himself back to the step. He'd give the car up in a heartbeat if it would turn the clock back, if it would change things. But it wouldn't.

Nothing he could do would achieve that. What

did a bit of dog hair matter in the grand scheme of things?

She moved to sit on the step below him. The dog remained where he was. 'I know it's scandalous, Mac—a dog in your precious car. But...'

'What are we doing with a dog, Jo?'

Her gaze drifted to his scar. He turned that side of his face away from her and pretended to stare out to sea.

'Is this some underhand attempt to provide me with pet therapy?'

She huffed out a breath. 'No.' She patted her knee. 'Come on, Bandit.' The dog remained sitting by the car. 'I... He's for me, not you, but I don't think he likes me very much.'

He glanced at her to find her frowning at the dog.

'Bandit's is a sad story...' She told it to him, and then said, 'So, you see, when Mr Cole's face lit up so much at my promise to bring Bandit to visit him *and* he started crying I had to take Bandit then and there. Mr Cole would've fretted and thought me no fit carer for Bandit if I'd insisted on getting The Beast rather than letting him ride in Beauty.'

She'd dubbed his car *Beauty*?

It certainly suited the car. And it suited the woman who'd just driven it.

'You do see that, don't you?'

He let out a breath and nodded.

She reached forward and clasped his hand briefly. 'Thank you.' She turned to survey the dog again.

He stared at the hand she'd clasped. He closed it to a fist and tried to stave off the warmth threatening to flood him.

'Do you think he doesn't like me because I'm so big?'

'You're not big!'

Astonished sage eyes stared into his.

He clicked his fingers. 'Bandit.'

The dog immediately rose and leapt up the steps to sit at Mac's feet. 'See—I'm bigger than you and he's fine with it.'

'But you're a man, and I'm big for a woman. I expect animals sense those kinds of things.'

'Nonsense.'

'He likes you.'

Her crestfallen face told him that she had indeed bought the dog for herself, and not some attempt to lure him out of whatever dark pit of depression she imagined him in.

'His previous owner was a man, so it only stands to reason that he's used to men.'

'I guess…'

'Besides, he'll be missing this Mr Cole of his and not understanding what's happening.'

'Oh, yes, the poor thing.' She reached out and gave the dog a gentle hug and a kiss to the top of his head.

Mac's heart started to thump when he imagined—

Don't imagine!

He cleared his throat and tried to clear his mind. 'Once he works out that you're the person who feeds him you'll win both his undying love and his loyalty.'

'Are dogs really that simple?' She gave a funny little grimace. 'I've never had one before.'

'Feed them and treat them with kindness and they'll love you. End of story. You just need to give him some adjustment time. I'd suggest you set him up a bed in the kitchen or the laundry, so he doesn't try and wander off at night to find his old home.' He shrugged at her questioning glance. 'Russ and I had dogs when we were growing up.'

'Thank you.'

She suddenly leaned away from him and it made him realise he'd been talking to her, facing her, with his scar in full view.

'What are you doing outside anyway? Were you

waiting for me to get back? Oh, I didn't worry you, did I? I didn't mean to be longer than twenty or thirty minutes but then—'

'Not at all.' His heart pounded. Hard. 'I was just going for a walk.' People went to hell for lying as well as he did.

She pressed a hand to her chest. Her lovely, generous chest.

'That's a relief. I was worried you'd think I'd made off with your fabulous car.' She bit her lip. 'I don't suppose Bandit and I could come on that walk too?'

What could he say to that? He glanced out at the beckoning sea, the field of winter grass and wild native flowers, noted the way the breeze rippled through it all and how the sun shone with winter mildness and tried not to let it filter into him, relax him…gladden him.

'Sure.'

'I suspect, though, that you should wear a sunhat to protect you…' She touched the left side of her face to indicate that she meant his burn scar. 'From sunburn.'

He should.

'You go get a hat and I'll put Beauty in the garage.'

They both rose. Bandit looked at Mac expectantly. Her face fell almost comically.

'You're not taking that fleabag in my car again,' he said to mediate her disappointment at the dog's reaction.

'So much for "It's just a car, Jo",' she muttered, but her lips twitched as she said it. She patted Bandit on the head. 'You be a good boy. I'll be back soon.'

She folded herself into the car and her face broke into the biggest grin when she started it up again. She touched the accelerator just for fun and the car roared in instant response.

He turned on his heel and strode through the house to hide his sudden laughter. 'Bandit, I hope one day your new mistress gets herself her dream car. She'll know exactly how to enjoy it.'

Bandit wagged his tail, following Mac all the way through the house and up to his bedroom.

Mac rifled through drawers, looking for a hat. 'Don't look at me like that, dog. I'm not your master. *She* is.'

Bandit just wagged his tail harder. Mac shook his head and slathered sunscreen across his face. What on earth did Jo think she was going to do with a dog?

She was waiting on the veranda when he finally returned. She wore a basketball cap. 'I always have one in The Beast,' she explained when he glanced at it. 'Sunstroke is no laughing matter on a survey camp.'

'It's not a laughing matter anywhere, is it?'

She shrugged and pulled her hand from behind her back to reveal a tennis ball. Bandit started to bark.

'He came amply provided for.'

With that, she threw the ball and Bandit hurtled after it. She set off after him, turning back after four or five strides.

'Well? Aren't you coming?'

The previous two days he'd walked the property line behind the house and away from the sea. With an internal curse he kicked himself into action, trying not to let the holiday spirit infect him. But when Bandit came back and dropped the ball at Mac's feet and Jo gave a snort of disgust all he could do was laugh.

'Shut up and throw the ball for the ungrateful bag of bones.'

So he did.

They walked down a steeply inclined field, and then across level ground, and the whole time Mac tried to ignore the scent of the sea and the tug of the breeze caressing his face and the feeling of ease that tried to invade him. He hadn't realised it but he'd grown cramped in the house these last few weeks, and moving now was like releasing a pent-up sigh.

He didn't deserve to enjoy any of it.

He slammed to a halt. But it was going to prove necessary if he was to remain healthy. Jo was right about that. And he had to remain healthy. He had a debt to pay off.

'Are you okay?'

That warm honey voice flowed over him, somehow intensifying the sun's warmth and the silk of the breeze.

'Not tired out already, are you?'

He kicked forward again. 'Of course not.' That wasn't to say that the hill on the way back wasn't going to give him a run for his money. 'I'm just...'

'Yes?'

'I'm just trying to figure out the best way to apologise for my behaviour on Monday, when you arrived.'

'Ah.' She marched up a low sand dune.

He didn't want to go onto the beach. He hadn't guarded his privacy so fiercely to blow his cover now. As if sensing his reluctance, she found a flat patch of sand amongst a riot of purple pigface and sat to watch as Bandit raced down to the water's edge to chase waves. After a moment's hesitation he sat beside her. He kept his right side towards her.

'You *were* expecting me on Monday, weren't you?'

'Yes.'

'Then why the foul temper? You didn't seriously expect to live under the same roof as someone and manage to avoid them completely, did you?'

Had he? He wasn't sure, but he could see now what a ludicrous notion that was. 'I've obviously fallen into bad habits. It wasn't deliberate, and it certainly wasn't the object of the exercise.'

'By *exercise* I suppose you're referring to holing up out here in royal isolation? What's the object?'

'The object is to write this darn cookbook, and I was having a particularly rough day with it on Monday.'

She let out a breath. 'And I waltzed in like a…'

'Like a cyclone.'

'Wreaking havoc and destruction.'

'And letting in the fresh air.'

She turned to stare at him. His mouth went

dry but he forced himself to continue. 'You were right. I've been shutting myself up for days on end, hardly setting foot outside, and some days barely eating. If you hadn't shown up and shaken me up I'd have been in grave danger of falling ill. And I can assure you that's *not* what I want.'

He wasn't on a suicide mission.

He readied himself for a grilling—did he mean what he said or was he trying to manipulate her for Russ's benefit, et cetera, et cetera?

Instead she turned to him, her gaze steady. 'Why is the cookbook so important?'

CHAPTER FOUR

WAS THE COOKBOOK a way for Mac to take his mind off the fact he no longer had a television show? No longer had a job? His fisted hands and clenched jaw told her it consumed him, and not necessarily in a good way.

When he didn't answer she tried again. 'What's the big deal with the cookbook, Mac?'

He finally turned to look at her. 'Money.'

'You have a deal with a publisher?'

He gave a single nod before he turned back to stare at the sea.

'If you hate it that much—' and she was pretty certain he did '—can't you just…?' She shrugged. She didn't know how these things worked. 'Change your mind? Apologise and pay back the advance?'

'You don't understand.'

Obviously not.

'I *need* the money.'

She had no hope of hiding her surprise, but she did what she could to haul her jaw back into place in super-quick time. 'But you must've made a truckload of money from your TV show.'

Not to mention all those guest appearances and endorsements. Still, if he'd gone around buying expensive cars willy-nilly she supposed he might have burned through it pretty quickly. Not that it was any of her business. And it wasn't any of Russ's business either.

'I… Sorry, I just thought you were rolling in it.'

'I was.'

So what on earth had he done with it all?

She had no intention of asking, but possibilities circled through her mind—bad investments, gambling, living the high life with no thought for the future.

'It's all gone on medical bills.'

That had her swinging back. 'Yours was a workplace accident.' It had occurred during the filming of one of his TV episodes. 'Insurance should've taken care of the medical expenses.'

'Not *my* medical bills, Jo. The money hasn't gone on *my* medical bills.'

A world of weariness stretched through his voice. And then it hit her. That young apprentice who'd also been involved in the fire. 'Ethan?' she whispered.

He didn't respond with either a yea or a nay.

She rubbed a hand across her forehead, re-adjusted her cap. 'But the insurance should've covered his medical expenses too. I—'

He swung to her, his eyes blazing. 'He's still in hospital! He still has to wear a bodysuit. His family wanted to move him to a private facility, where he'd get the best of care, but they couldn't afford the fees.'

Living the high life with no thought for tomorrow? Oh, how wrong she'd been!

She reached out to clasp his arm. 'Oh, Mac...' He'd taken on so much.

He shook her off and leapt to his feet. She pulled her hands into her lap, stung. A man like Mac would resent the sympathy of a woman like her.

Striking, huh? *Yeah, right.*

He spun to her, lips twisting. 'Who should pay but me? *I'm* the reason he's lying in a hospital bed with second-and third-degree burns to sixty per cent of his body. I've ruined that young man's life. I'm the guilty party. So the least I can do is—'

'What a load of codswallop!' She shot to her feet too. 'If we want to take this right down to brass tacks it's the producers and directors of your television show who should be paying in blood.'

Kitchen Encounters, as Mac's television show had been called, had followed the day-to-day dramas of Mac's catering team as they'd gone from event to event—a charity dinner with minor royalty one week, a wedding the next, then perhaps a gala awards night for some prestigious sporting event. Throughout it all Mac had been portrayed as loud, sweary and exacting—an over-the-top, demanding perfectionist. So over the top that even if Jo hadn't had the inside line from Russ she'd have known it was all for show—for the ratings, for the spectacle it created.

That wasn't how the press had portrayed it after the accident, though. They'd condemned Mac's behaviour and claimed the *Kitchen Encounters* set had been an accident waiting to happen. All nonsense. But such nonsense sold newspapers in the same way that conflict and drama sold TV shows.

Mac remained silent. He fell back to the sand, his shoulders slumping in a way that made her heart twist. Standing above him like this made her conscious of her height. She sat again, but a little further away this time, in the hope she wouldn't do something stupid like reach out and touch him again.

She moistened her lips. 'Russ told me that the

persona you adopted for the show was fake—that it was what the producers demanded. He also said everyone on the show was schooled in their reactions too.'

Conflicts carefully orchestrated, as in any fictional show or movie, to create drama, to create good guys and bad guys. Some weeks Mac had played the darling and others the villain. It had led to compulsive viewing.

'The accident wasn't your fault. You were playing the role you were assigned. You weren't the person who dropped a tray of oysters and ice into a pot of hot oil.' That had been Ethan. 'It was an accident.' A terrible, tragic accident.

'For God's sake, Jo, I was yelling at him—bellowing at him to hurry up. He was nineteen years old, it was only his second time on the show, and he was petrified.'

He didn't yell or bellow now. He spoke quietly, but there was a savage edge to his words that she suspected veiled a wealth of pain.

'He was acting. Just like you were.'

'No.'

He turned and those eyes lasered through her. Blond hair the colour of sand, blue eyes the colour of the sea, and olive skin that was still too pale.

His beauty hit her squarely in the chest, making it hard to breathe.

'He was truly petrified. I just didn't realise until it was too late.'

She gripped her hands tightly in her lap to stop them from straying. 'From all accounts if you hadn't acted so quickly to smother the fire Ethan would be dead.' The other actors on the set had labelled Mac a hero.

'He hasn't thanked me for that, Jo.'

It took a moment for her to realise what he meant. She stared out to sea and blinked hard, swallowing the lump that was doing its best to lodge in her throat.

'Do you know how painful his treatment is? It's like torture.'

'He's young,' she managed to whisper. 'One day this will all be behind him.'

'And he'll be disfigured for life. All because I played the game the TV producers wanted—all because I was hungry for ratings and success and acclaim. At any time I could've said no. I could've demanded that we remain true to the "reality" part of our so-called reality show. I could've demanded that everyone on set be treated with courtesy and respect.'

If he had, she suspected the show wouldn't have lasted beyond a single season.

'I didn't. I chose not to.'

There was nothing wrong with wanting to be successful, with wanting praise and applause for a job well done. If anyone took a poll she'd bet ninety-nine per cent of the population wanted those things too.

'My pursuit of ratings has ruined a boy's life.'

And now he was doing all he could to make amends, to make Ethan's life as comfortable as he could. She shuddered to think how expensive those medical bills must be. She didn't believe for a moment that Mac should hold himself responsible, but neither did she believe she had any hope of changing his mind on that.

What a mess!

One thing seemed certain, though. If he didn't ease up he'd become ill. At least he seemed to recognise that fact now.

Or was that just a clever manipulation on his behalf so she wouldn't go telling tales to Russ?

She glanced at Mac from the corner of her eye as Bandit came racing up from the beach, tongue lolling out and fur wet from the surf. He collapsed at Mac's feet, looking the epitome of happy, satisfied dog. If only she could get a similarly contented expression on Mac's face her job here would be done.

Unbidden, an image punched through her, so raunchy that she started to choke. That *wasn't* what she'd meant! She leapt to her feet and strode a few steps away. Mac would laugh his head off if he could read her mind at the moment.

Laughter is good for the soul.

Yeah, well, in this instance it would shrivel hers.

She put the image out of her mind, pulled in a breath and turned to face him. His gaze was fixed on her hips. He stared for another two beats before he started. Colour slashed high across his cheekbones.

Had he been checking out her butt?

She wiped her hands down her jeans. Ridiculous notion.

But he couldn't meet her gaze, and then she couldn't meet his. She stared up at the sky. 'So what's the problem you've been having with your recipes?'

'They're complicated.'

'Naturally. It's one of the reasons your show was so gripping. There seemed to be so many things that could go wrong with each individual dish.'

'I promised the publisher a troubleshooting section for each recipe.'

That sounded challenging.

'I'm not a writer!' He dragged both hands back through his hair. 'This stuff—the explanations—doesn't come naturally to me. I don't know if they're coherent, let alone if a lay person could follow them.'

And if he refused to actually cook the dishes then how much harder was he making this on himself? He'd always proclaimed himself an instinctive chef. Just getting the order right of when to do what must be a nightmare.

It hit her then. How she could help him. And how he could help her.

She moistened her lips. 'Why don't you give me the drafts of your recipes and we'll see if I can make them? See if they make sense to me?'

She shifted her gaze to Bandit—it was easier than looking at Mac—but she couldn't help but notice how Mac's feet stilled where they'd been rubbing against Bandit's back.

'You'd do that?'

Forcing in a breath, she met his gaze. His eyes held hope, and something else she couldn't decipher. 'I'll try, but you have to understand that I'm no cook.'

'You're the perfect demographic.'

She was?

'A plain cook who wants to branch out and try her hand at something new—something more complicated and exotic.'

That wasn't her at all. She just wanted to learn how to make a *macaron* tower.

'This would help me out. A lot.'

And her too, she hoped. He might refuse to stand side by side with her in a kitchen and show her how to make fiddly little *macarons*, but he might be worked on to create a sensible, within the realms of possible, *macaron* recipe for her.

'If you're sure?' he added.

So much for the demanding, overbearing kitchen tyrant. Russ had always chortled at Mac's on-air tantrums. She was starting to see why.

'As long as you're prepared to eat the odd disaster for dinner if things don't always work out.'

'What the heck? We've always got fish fingers to fall back on.'

She laughed.

'What if I give you the first recipe tomorrow?'

She nodded. And then glanced around at the

lengthening shadows and shivered a little. The warmth quickly leached from the air as the afternoon closed in.

'Speaking of dinner, I'll need to get back and start it soon.' The beef stew she'd planned needed to simmer for at least an hour and a half.

'And I should get a bit more work done.'

He moved to get up and she started to offer him her hand, and then snatched it back, remembering the way he'd shaken off her touch earlier.

Mac's gaze narrowed and he leant back on his hands, peering up at her from beneath the brim of his hat. 'Did my lascivious gaze earlier embarrass you?'

She almost swallowed her tongue. His *what*? So he *had* been…? Was he saying…? Surely not!

'Of course not,' she lied.

He rose to his feet in one smooth motion. Bandit immediately leapt to his feet too. 'I did tell you that you were a striking woman.'

She snorted and turned towards the house. 'You've been stuck out here on your own for too long.'

Without warning, cool, firm fingers gripped the suddenly overheated flesh of her forearm, pulling her to a halt. 'And you're selling yourself short.'

No, she wasn't. She just knew what she was. And she wasn't the kind of woman who turned men's heads. Mac was just trying to charm her, manipulate her.

'I should put your mind at rest, though.' He stroked her skin with his index finger before releasing her. 'I want to assure you that you're perfectly safe from unwanted attention. I have no intention of thrusting myself on you. I do mean to act like a perfect gentleman towards you, Jo.'

She wished he hadn't used the term *thrusting*.

She drew herself up to her full height but he still towered over her. 'No other scenario occurred to me, I assure you.'

'Good.' His eyes twinkled for a moment. 'It doesn't mean I can't enjoy looking at you, though.'

Jo stumbled. Mac laughed. Bandit barked and raced off towards the house.

Mac paced back and forth outside the kitchen door.

Jo peered around the doorway. 'You *can* come in and watch, you know. You could sit at the table.'

If he did that he'd bark instructions at her the moment she started. He'd make her nervous and she'd have an accident and burn herself. His stomach churned at the thought. If he sat in the kitchen he wouldn't be able to resist the temptation to take over.

He didn't deserve to indulge his passion when a boy lay in a hospital bed, suffering because of that passion.

'So, all I'm doing at the moment is infusing these few ingredients for the béarnaise sauce I'm to make tonight, right?

'That's right.'

'And—'

'No questions,' he ordered. 'I need to know if you can follow the recipe.'

'Okay—gotcha.'

He couldn't have said why, but her earnest expression made him want to kiss her.

He could just imagine how she'd recoil from *that*. He grimaced, and tried to push the thought from his mind, but it didn't stop the itch and burn that coursed through his body.

'If you're not going to watch then you best go somewhere else to pace. You're making me nervous.'

Go where? Do what? He didn't have a hope of settling to work at the moment. What if she didn't understand an instruction? What if—?

'Go toss a ball for Bandit.'

With a nod, he barrelled outside. The dog had a seemingly boundless reserve of energy.

Mac threw the ball three times. When Bandit brought it back the third time he gave the border collie an absent-minded scratch behind the ears. 'How do you think she's getting on in there, boy?'

He glanced back towards the house. It wasn't as if she had to do anything difficult—just measure out a few ingredients, chop up a tablespoon of onion. Simple, right?

He sprang up the steps and moved soundlessly across to the door. He breathed in deeply but couldn't smell anything. He straightened, ran a hand back through his hair. He should at least smell the vinegar being brought to the boil by now, surely? She should be reducing the mixture and…

Maybe she hadn't started the reduction yet.

He reached for the door handle.

Bandit barked.

With a curse, Mac wheeled away and clattered back down the steps. He threw the ball until his arm grew tired and then he switched arms. Bandit didn't show any signs of tiring. All the while Mac kept his attention cocked for any sign of sound and movement behind him.

Finally Jo emerged from the front door, bearing a plate of sandwiches, a jug of water and two glasses. 'Hungry?' she called out.

Not a bit—but he moved to where she'd set the things on the wooden table that stood at one end of the veranda and poured them both glasses of water. He drank his in an effort to appear nonchalant.

'Run into any problems?'

She settled on the bench that sat between the living room windows, bit into a sandwich and lifted one shoulder.

He peered at her sandwich and blinked. 'Is that peanut butter and honey?'

'Yup.'

He stared.

'What?' She glared. 'I *like* peanut butter and honey. You don't have to eat one. I made you roast beef and pickles.'

He obeyed the unspoken demand in her voice and selected a sandwich. 'What did the shrug mean?' He promptly bit into the sandwich to stop himself pressing her further.

She licked a drizzle of honey from her fingers. It was unconsciously sensuous and very seductive. The fact that she didn't mean it to be didn't make a scrap of difference. He forced his gaze away and concentrated on chewing and swallowing.

'I think I should probably tell you that I'm not up on a lot of cooking terminology. The very first time a recipe told me to *"cream the butter and sugar"* I thought it was directing me to add cream to the butter and sugar.'

He'd been leaning with a hip against the railing but he surged upright at her words. 'This recipe didn't ask you to cream anything.'

She waved a hand through the air. 'That's just an example. But…you know…*"reduce the mixture by a third"* isn't the kind of thing I read every day.'

'Do you think I need to add an explanation to describe what reducing means?'

She pursed her lips. 'No, I figured it out, but…'

He leaned towards her. 'Yes?'

'Why go to all the trouble of reducing at all? Why not just add less vinegar, water and onion to begin with?'

'Simmering the ingredients together infuses the flavours to provide a base for the sauce.'

She sat back and stared. 'Now *that's* interesting.' She pointed a finger at him. 'That should go in the cookbook.'

Really?

'But, you know, I want you to realise that I might be more clueless than your real demographic, so—'

'No, you're perfect.'

She glanced up, obviously startled at this statement. Their gazes locked for a moment. They both glanced away at the same time.

Mac's heart surged against his ribs. Why did this woman have to affect him like this? He'd known beautiful women in the past who had left him cold. Why couldn't Jo leave him cold?

Oh, no, not her. She threatened to ignite him. And for the first time in months the thought of heat and fire didn't fill his soul with dread. He glanced back at her. The pulse at the base of her throat fluttered madly. Unlike him, though, it wouldn't be desire but fear that had sent the blood surging through her veins. Fear that he would touch her.

It left a bad taste in his mouth.

'So…' She cleared her throat. 'My reduction is cooling and infusing, and I'll strain it later when I'm ready to make the sauce. Feel free to go and check it out.'

He started for the door.

'But…'

He turned back.

'I didn't know what tarragon vinegar was.'

He strode back to where she sat, one eyebrow raised.

'So I just used plain old white vinegar.'

He let out a breath.

'I briefly flirted with the idea of adding a herb to the mixture—like rosemary.'

He grimaced. It wouldn't be the end of the world, but—

'Though in the end I decided not to risk it.'

'It sounds as if you've done a great job.'

She didn't look convinced. 'I have another request to make. I've no idea what a double saucepan is.'

She needed to use one when adding butter—bit by tiny bit—to the reduction later, to create the sauce.

'I'm not asking you to tell me what it is, but can I bring my laptop into the kitchen with me? I would if I were cooking at home.'

'Of course you can.'

'And the final thing,' she said before he could walk away again. 'This recipe is Steak with Béarnaise Sauce, but you haven't said what you want served with it.'

'New potatoes and green beans.'

'Then you might want to include that at the end of the recipe too.'

Good point.

She suddenly laughed. 'I can see you're itching to check it out, so go. But wash your hands first. I don't want dog hair in my reduction.'

He raced into the kitchen. He washed and dried his hands and then moved to the small saucepan sitting on the stovetop. He could tell at a glance that she'd used too much onion. He lifted the saucepan to his nose and sniffed. It was a pity about the tarragon vinegar—if she was happy to continue this experiment of theirs then they'd need to stock up on some of the more exotic ingredients—but all in all she'd done okay. The tension bled out of his shoulders.

She glanced up when he stepped back out onto the veranda. 'Well?'

'You've done a fine job. It's not exactly how I'd want it, which tells me what parts of my instructions I need to fine-tune.'

Elation suddenly coursed through him. He could make this work. He *could*! Then there'd be enough money for Ethan's hospital bills for the foreseeable future.

And after that?

He pushed that thought away. He had every intention of making sure Ethan was looked after for the rest of his life. Maybe he could do a whole series of cookbooks if this one sold well?

'This was a brilliant idea of yours, Jo. I can't thank you enough.'

She waved that away.

'If there's anything I can do in return…?'

She glanced up. The sage in her eyes deepened for a moment. 'I believe you mean that.'

'I *do* mean it.' He'd have sat on the bench beside her, but that would mean sitting with the left side of his face towards her. He leant against the railing again instead.

'Hold that thought.'

She disappeared into the house. She returned a moment later with a picture. His heart sank when she handed it to him. It was that damned *macaron* tower she'd already mentioned.

'*Macarons* are tricky.'

'Yes, but could you write me a recipe telling me how to make them—how to make that?'

He blew out a breath. 'This is an advanced recipe.'

'But practice makes perfect, right? I have plenty of time on my hands. I'll just keep practising.'

'Why do you want to make a *macaron* tower?' He could name a hundred tastier desserts.

He handed her back the picture. She took it, but a bad taste stretched through him when he realised how careful she was not to touch him.

She stared down at the picture before folding it in half. 'My grandmother turns eighty-five in two months, one week, four days and—what?—eleven hours twenty minutes? I've promised to make her one of these.'

Wow.

'I want to do something nice for her.'

'Nice' would be taking her flowers, or treating her to lunch at a decent restaurant. *Or making her a* macaron *tower.*

'Please, Mac, don't look like that! This *has* to be possible. I'm not that much of a klutz in the kitchen. This is something I can build up to.'

'Of course you can.'

'He says with fake jollity,' she said, so drily he had to laugh.

'I didn't mean that you can't do it. I'm just blown away by the fact you *want* to.'

'I love my grandmother. I want to do something that will make her happy. She's as fit as a horse, and as sharp as a tack, but she's still coming up to eighty-five.'

She rose and seized the other half of her peanut

butter and honey sandwich and came to lean beside him on the railing, on his left side. He turned to stare out to sea, giving her his right side instead.

'My grandmother and my great-aunt raised me. Their relationship has always been tempestuous. My grandmother always praised me and indulged me. My great-aunt always thought it in my best interests to…um…not to do that.'

He stilled and glanced at her, but he couldn't read her face.

'There's an ongoing dispute over the rightful ownership of my great-grandmother's pearl necklace. My great-aunt scoffed at the idea of my making that *macaron* tower and I'm afraid my grandmother has staked the pearl necklace on the fact that I can.'

His jaw dropped.

'I believe my so-called *womanly* qualities have always been in dispute, and I'm afraid my great-aunt is now convinced that the necklace is hers.'

He straightened. 'What exactly does she mean by *womanly* qualities?' As far as he could see Jo's 'womanly qualities' were exemplary. 'You mean the domestic arts?'

She pointed what was left of her sandwich at him. 'Exactly.'

He reached around her for another sandwich. It brought him in close. She smelled faintly of onions, vinegar and honey. His mouth watered. He ached to reach across, touch his lips to her cheek to see what she tasted like.

Jo polished off the rest of her sandwich and pushed away from the railing to amble down the veranda a little way before turning. 'I don't mean to give up without a fight.'

He turned to face the house again, presenting her with his good side. 'I can understand that.' But didn't she resent being piggy in the middle between the two older women?

'Why do you keep doing that?'

A chill fluttered through him. 'Doing what?'

'Keeping the right side of your face towards me? Isn't it tiring?'

CHAPTER FIVE

IT WAS REALLY starting to bug her, the way Mac tried to hide his scar. Jo understood physical self-consciousness all too well, but Mac couldn't spend the rest of his life trying to hide one side of his face. It just wouldn't work.

'The way you're going, you'll give yourself whip-lash.'

'I have no idea what you're talking about.'

How cold he could sound when he wanted—but she knew better. Mac wasn't cold. He was… Well, he was hot. But that wasn't what she meant.

He was devoting his life to making Ethan Devlin's life better. Those weren't the actions of a cold man.

'Really?' she said, walking around to his left side and deliberately surveying his scars. She'd noticed them before, of course, but scars didn't make the man, and she'd had other issues with Mac that had nothing to do with what he looked like.

The scars were red and angry. She sucked in a breath. Heck, they must hurt!

The pulse at the base of his jaw pounded. He held his body taut, as if it were taking all his strength to remain where he stood, and let her look at him.

He finally turned to glare at her, eyes flashing and lips pressed into a thin line. 'Satisfied?'

She stared back at him and had to swallow. Mac, when he was riled like this, was pretty virile. She had a feeling that the glare, the set of those shoulders and the angle of his jaw were all supposed to have her shaking in her boots. *Uh, no.* Though it certainly had her pulse racing. She moistened her lips. What it really made her want to do was run *to* him—not away from him.

Lord, wouldn't he laugh if he knew?

'I don't precisely know what you mean by *satisfied*, Mac.'

He swung away to stare out to sea, presenting her with his 'good' side again. 'Satisfied,' he growled, 'as in have you had your fill of looking at it?'

Oh.

He kept his gaze firmly fixed in front of him, but she had a feeling he didn't see the glorious view—the cobalt sky, the indigo and aquamarine of the sea, the white foam of the surf and the golden beach, all at their most vivid at this time of the year before the sun bleached everything pale with summer intensity.

'Doesn't it sicken you to look at it?'

Her head rocked back. 'Of course not.'

He turned to glare, a blast of arctic chill from frigid eyes. 'When you first arrived you said these scars shocked you to the core. Those were your exact words.'

She drew herself upright. 'I wasn't referring to your scars, you stupid—' She bit back something rude and vulgar. 'I was referring to how much you'd let yourself go!'

His jaw dropped.

She reached out and poked him in the shoulder. 'Don't you *dare* accuse me of being so shallow.'

His shoulders unbent.

She frowned and adjusted her stance. 'Does it sicken *you* whenever you look in a mirror?'

One of those lovely shoulders lifted. 'I'm used to it.'

'But what? You don't think anyone else can get used to it? You don't think anyone else can see past it?'

He didn't say anything.

'I've met beautiful people who've proved to be

spiteful or selfish or snobs, and suddenly I find their allure loses most of its gloss. I have friends who may not fit society's rigid ideal of beautiful, but they have such good hearts I think them the most beautiful people in the world.'

'Jo, I—'

'No! You listen to what I have to say! If you value yourself and others only through physical beauty then you deserve to suffer every torment imaginable at the thought of losing your so-called pretty face. But, as far as your face is concerned, I think it's as pretty as it ever was.'

He stilled. He stared at her for a long moment. 'You really mean that?'

She did.

He dragged in a breath and then turned to lean against the railing, his left side towards her. 'I'm sorry I insinuated…' He glanced at her. 'That you were shallow. I didn't mean to.' He paused. 'I agree that a person's attractiveness is more than how they look, but…'

She tried not to focus on the languid line of his body. 'But…?'

'There's no denying looks have an impact on how a person is perceived.'

'If a person is repelled by your scars they're not

worth the time of day.' She folded her arms. 'You know, it could prove a useful filtering device.'

He gave a bark of laughter. 'You can't say that.'

'Don't let anyone know you feel self-conscious about it, Mac. That's my best advice. They'll see it as a weakness, and there are people in the world who pounce on others' weaknesses in an effort to build themselves up.'

He turned to her more fully. 'That sounds like the voice of experience.'

She shrugged and tried to walk the walk she'd just talked. 'Look at me.' She gestured down at herself.

'I've been doing my very best not to do that, Jo. I promised you gentlemanly behaviour, but when I look at you…'

She rolled her eyes. '*Do* be serious.'

Mac moved to trap her against the veranda post and the side of the house. He planted one hand on the weatherboards by her head, the other on the railing near her waist. Her mouth dried. Her heart thudded so hard she found it impossible to catch her breath.

'What on earth do you think you're—?'

'Shut up or I'll kiss you.'

She almost swallowed her tongue.

'You have the nerve to give me a lecture about shallowness, beauty and an individual's true worth, and then you want to carry on with *you're not attractive*?'

She opened her mouth. His eyes suddenly gleamed, fixing on her mouth with a hunger that had to be feigned! But she remembered his threat and snapped her mouth shut.

'What a shame,' he murmured, and in his eyes was a mixture of laughter and regret.

She wanted to call him a liar, but she didn't dare.

'When I said you were a striking woman I meant that in every positive way there is. I meant that I find you attractive. I meant that it takes a Herculean effort on my part whenever I look at you to conceal my desire.'

She choked.

'And it's not because I've been isolated for the last four months.'

Again, she was tempted to call him a liar. She was tempted to say anything that would make him kiss her. Warmth threaded through her stomach at the thought, her thighs softened and her breasts grew heavy.

But if he kissed her she wouldn't be able to help it. She'd kiss him back and then he'd know how much she wanted him, how attractive she found him, and it would make her vulnerable. She swallowed. She didn't want to be vulnerable around this man.

'You seem to think you're too tall for a woman...'

He moved in closer, his heat swamping her, though he still didn't touch her. He smelled of soap and freshly ironed cotton...and very faintly of dog. She really wished that last would put her off, but it didn't.

'I don't think you're too tall. I think you and I would fit perfectly.'

They might not be touching, but this close to him she felt dwarfed.

'I could stare into your eyes all day. They're so clear, and the colour changes depending on your emotion. I find myself wanting to learn what each shade means.'

That voice of his, its low intimate tone and the words he uttered, could weave a spell around a woman.

He eased back a fraction and she managed to draw air into her lungs again. Until she realised what he was doing and the breath jammed in her throat again.

'You have the most intriguingly womanly shape—all dips and curves.'

He was staring at her body the same way she'd stared at his face a short while ago. Had *he* felt this exposed? For heaven's sake, she was fully clothed, but Mac's eyes were practically undressing her—as if he was imagining what she'd look like without said clothes—and his eyes started to gleam and he actually licked his lips. She swallowed a moan and sagged against the wall, her pulse racing, bustling, jumping.

'Your body is lush and strong, and I'd be a liar if I said I wasn't aching to explore it. Thoroughly and intensely.'

The words scraped out of him, a hoarse whisper, and Jo's head fell back against the house as she struggled to draw air into her lungs.

'But that's just the outside packaging. The woman I'm getting to know is passionate, she gives no quarter, but she is remarkably generous.'

His gaze burned fiercely down into hers. She couldn't have uttered a word if her life had depended on it.

'And all of that makes me ache that much more to make love with you.'

How on earth had the morning descended to

this? For years she'd worked among teams of men in remote locations in the Outback and she'd always managed to keep things on a professional footing.

This was only her fifth day with Mac, and the air was charged with so much blatant sensuality it would melt anyone foolish enough to stumble into its path.

'But I promised to be gentlemanly, so I won't, but I'm sick to death of this ridiculous belief of yours that you're not attractive. You're a beautiful and very desirable woman.'

It frightened her. *He* frightened her. Because she wanted to believe him. Yet in her heart she knew it was all lies.

Mac eased away and she tossed her head. 'I know my worth, Mac, make no mistake. I'm smart and strong and I'm a good friend. But let's make one thing very clear. Boys like you do *not* kiss girls like me.' Not unless it was for a bet or a dare, or they were trying to manipulate them in some way. 'It's a fact of life.' A fact she had no intention of forgetting.

He'd started to turn away, but now he turned back, a flare of anger darkening his face. And then a slow, satisfied gleam lit his eyes, his mouth, even his shoulders—though she couldn't have explained how.

'Perfect…' he crooned.

And then he moved in.

She raised her hands. 'Don't you—'

He claimed her lips swiftly, pushing her back against the house, taking his time exploring every inch of her mouth. She tried to turn her head to the side, but he followed her, his hands cupping her face. He crowded her completely, pressing every inch of his rock-hard self against her. His chest flattened her breasts—breasts that strained to get closer. He thrust a leg between her thighs, pressing against her most sensitive spot in the most irresistible way. It made her gasp. With a purr of satisfaction his tongue plundered her mouth.

Stop! Stop! Stop!

But he didn't stop kissing her, savouring her, pressing against her, making her feel desired, making her feel beautiful, and with a moan scraping from the back of her throat she curled her hands into the soft cotton of his sweater and kissed him back. She wanted to know him, taste him. She wanted to savour him in the same way he savoured her. Her hands explored his shoulders and dived into the thickness of his hair. But she wanted more—so much more.

One of his arms went around her waist—he spanned it effortlessly—and hauled her closer as if she weighed nothing. It sent shivers of delight spiralling through her. Their kisses went from tasting and savouring to a deepening hunger. Held in his arms like this, dwarfed by his height and breadth, Jo felt almost dainty, utterly feminine and beautiful.

When his hand slid beneath her shirt to cup her breast his moan made her shake. He was moaning for *her*. He wanted *her*!

His thumb flicked across her nipple through the nylon of her bra. Desire spiked from her nipple to the core deep at the centre of her. She shifted against him, restless for more, seeking relief… seeking release and—

If they kept this up there was only one way it would end. She stilled. So did he. He didn't remove his hand from her breast and his heat branded her, tormented her. She didn't remove her arms from around his neck.

They both breathed hard, as if they'd run a race. 'I beg to differ.'

She blinked up at him blankly.

'Guys like me most certainly *do* kiss women like you. And what's more, Jo, they enjoy every moment of it.'

One kiss couldn't erase a lifetime of taunts, a lifetime of feeling she'd never measured up. A lifetime of never feeling beautiful.

She swallowed. Mac had kissed her as if he found her beautiful, but she still wasn't convinced he wasn't playing some deeper game. She removed her arms from around his neck. With the wall of his house behind her, she had nowhere to move to.

'Let me go, Mac.'

He did immediately.

Regardless of any of his reasons for kissing her, regardless of how much her body clamoured otherwise, this couldn't go any further.

'I've known you for five days.' Not even five full days. 'I don't jump into bed with men I've known for such a short time.' Was that his style?

He moved down to the next veranda post, leaving a whole span of veranda railing between them. 'I'm forty years old, Jo. The days when I thought one-night stands and flings were fun are long behind me.'

She'd never thought one-night stands or flings fun. Sharing her body with a man had always been a fraught experience and not one she'd ever raced into.

And yet today she'd almost…

She bent at the waist to lean her forearms along the railing, unconsciously mimicking Mac's posture.

'That kiss became a whole lot more a whole lot quicker than I meant it to,' he said.

She winced at the apology, glanced at him from the corner of her eye and found him staring stolidly out to sea. She grimaced, shuffled, and finally gave in, huffing out a breath. 'Yeah, well, it takes two to tango. It was just as much my fault as yours.'

He straightened and surveyed her. She tried not to picture what he must see—a clumsy giant of a woman. She remained in what she desperately hoped was a nonchalant, casual pose—a pose that proclaimed a kiss like that *hadn't* rocked her world. That kisses like that happened to her all the time and she was used to them.

Ha! If kisses like that happened to her all the time she'd be…

A very satisfied woman.

You mean a nervous wreck.

'I don't want to give you the wrong signals, Jo.'

She turned her head to stare at him. *Oh, right. Here it comes.* Inside, she started to shrivel.

'I'm not in the market for a fling. At twenty I thought such things could be uncomplicated, but I don't believe that any more. And I'm not in the market for a relationship. My life is already too complicated. A relationship would be one complication too many.' He swallowed and shuffled his feet. 'I...uh...hope you're okay with that.'

Men really were the most arrogant creatures. She straightened. 'Well, it might surprise you to hear that I'm not in the market for a relationship either—and I can't possibly imagine what gave you the idea that I was.'

He glared. 'You decided you had room in your life for a dog. It seems only logical a boyfriend would be next.'

Her jaw dropped. She hauled it back into place. She opened her mouth, then with a shake of her head snapped it shut. She moved to the door instead. 'I'm sure there's cleaning I should be doing.'

'So, we're okay?' Mac asked as she reached the door.

She folded her arms and turned. 'I don't know what *we* you're referring to, but I can tell you one thing—if I *were* in the market for a boyfriend, Mac, it wouldn't be with a man like you.'

His eyes practically bugged from his head. All his life he'd probably had women falling over themselves for him. She had no intention of being one of them.

'This—' she gestured to the view and their surroundings '—is beyond beautiful. It's glorious. But you don't even seem to notice it, let alone appreciate it. You hide from life.' She'd had enough of hiding. 'Life's too short. I mean to live my life to the full and I'm not giving that up for any man.'

Not even for one as pretty as Mac.

'Then what the hell are you doing out here?'

'I'm having a breather—but I'm not hiding.' She flung out an arm. 'I relish that view every single moment I can. I'm learning to cook fancy French food. I'm adopting homeless dogs and driving fast cars. I suspect I've lived more in the last three days than you have in the last three months.'

He gaped at her.

There didn't seem to be much more to say so she whirled into the house and didn't stop until she came to the kitchen. And then she didn't know what to do. She'd already cleaned it after making that reduction.

She put the jars of honey and peanut butter that still stood on the table back into the pantry. She slammed her hands to her hips. She'd left the plate of sandwiches on the veranda, along with their glasses. She didn't feel like going back out there and facing him yet.

She could spout off all she liked about how she didn't want a relationship and she didn't do flings, but one look at the broad span of his shoulders and her blood surged, her thighs weakened and her resolve threatened to dissolve.

Almost against her will she tiptoed back down the hallway to the front door. She peered out through the screen door, but Mac was nowhere to be seen. With a sigh of relief she retrieved the dishes, spying Mac and Bandit halfway across the field leading down to the sand dunes and beach.

He moved with an unconscious grace and—

Argh! She stomped back into the house and then jumped when the hall phone—an ancient contraption—rang.

Russ, no doubt. She set the dishes on the floor and picked up the receiver. 'Hello?'

A quick intake of breath greeted her. 'Who are *you*?'

Jo blinked. Not Russ, then, but an angry female.

It hadn't occurred to her but, despite Mac's protestations, was there some woman waiting for him in the wings? Some woman he was dangling until—?

She shook her head. She might only have known him for a few days but that seemed seriously unlikely.

She cleared her throat. 'May I ask who's speaking, please?'

'This is Mrs Devlin.'

Jo rested back against the wall, her stomach twisting.

'You may have heard of my son, Ethan Devlin?'

The apprentice burned in the accident.

Jo closed her eyes. 'Yes, of course. I'm terribly sorry about what happened to your son, Mrs Devlin.'

'Put that low-life swine Mac on the phone.'

Mrs Devlin's bitterness threatened to burn a hole right through the receiver. Jo managed to swallow. 'I'm sorry, but he's not available at the moment. Can I take a message?'

'What do you mean, he's not there? He should be *working*! And who the hell are *you*, my girl? His fancy woman?'

Wow. Just…*wow*! 'My name is Jo Anderson and I'm Mac's housekeeper—*not* his girlfriend. I don't appreciate the insinuation and nor do I deserve your rudeness.'

The sudden silence almost deafened her. 'He doesn't deserve the luxury of a housekeeper,' Mrs Devlin said, though her voice had lost the worst of its edge. 'He doesn't deserve a moment of peace.'

Jo dragged a hand through her hair. If Mac had been bearing the brunt of this woman's bitterness then no wonder he'd been driving himself so hard. She saw it then, in that moment—Mac was punishing himself. He refused to notice the glorious views, he refused to engage in physical activity he found pleasurable, he shut himself off from the things he loved, like his car, his brother...his cooking.

Oh, Mac.

'He needs to send more money. Tell him that. Where is he anyway?'

'He's out walking the dog.' Not that it was any of her business.

'He has a *dog*?' Outrage laced her words.

'It's my dog. And, Mrs Devlin?' she said, before the other woman hung up. 'I... Look, Mac is working so hard he's in danger of becoming ill.'

'He *should* suffer!' the other woman yelled down

the line. 'He should suffer the way he's made other people suffer!'

Such venom. She understood Mrs Devlin's fear and concern for her son. She understood her fighting for the very best care he could get. But to blame Mac like this? It was wrong. So wrong.

To say as much would be pointless. Mrs Devlin didn't want to listen to reason. Not yet. But what if she was to become afraid that the cash cow might dry up?

Jo hauled in a breath, wishing her stomach would stop churning. 'If Mac does become ill, Mrs Devlin, the money for Ethan's care will dry up.'

'How dare you—?'

'All I'm doing is stating facts. You want Mac to suffer—that much is clear—but if he does get sick he won't be able to earn money.' Certainly not the kind of money they were talking about here. 'My job is to make sure he eats three square meals a day and gets out into the fresh air for some exercise. Basically, I just nag him. I doubt he enjoys it.'

But even after only a few days of this routine Mac was starting to look better.

'What are you trying to say to me?' the other woman asked stiffly.

'What I'm saying is that, for the moment at least,

you need to choose between your desire for revenge and your son's care. If you choose the latter
then I suggest you ease up on the venom for a bit.'

The phone was slammed down.

'Well…' She grimaced at the receiver before setting it back in place. 'That went well.'

Mac stomped across the fields. What on earth had
possessed him to kiss Jo? From the first moment
he'd clapped eyes on her he'd sensed that she'd be
dynamite, that given half a chance she'd blow his
life apart.

He clenched his hands to fists. That couldn't happen from a single kiss.

Except it hadn't been a single kiss but a full-on
necking session that had hurtled him back to his
teenage years, when he'd first discovered girls and
sex. Kissing Jo had shaken him to his absolute
foundations.

Bandit barked and spun in a circle—first one
way and then the other. 'Okay, okay,' he grum-
bled, moving towards the sand dunes. 'Go for a
swim, then.'

Bandit didn't need any further encouragement.
Mac settled at the same spot where he and Jo had
sat yesterday and raked both hands back through

his hair. Okay, so those kisses had rocked his foundations, but they hadn't toppled them. As long as he didn't kiss her again he'd be fine.

He gave a low laugh. Kiss her again? The look she'd flung at him before she'd flounced into the house had told him she'd squash him like a bug if he so much as tried. Man, how he'd like to take up that challenge—to make her sheath her claws, to stroke her until she purred and—

He swore. She made him want all the things he'd turned his back on—all the things he couldn't have.

Bandit, damp and sandy, raced up the beach to fling himself at Mac, leaping onto his lap and covering his face in sloppy dog kisses. The show of affection took Mac off guard, but he put his arms around the dog and held him close. It was a warm body, and at that moment Mac found he needed a warm body.

Eventually the dog settled beside him.

'So you've decided to love someone else, huh?' Mac scratched Bandit's back and the dog groaned his pleasure. 'You should've chosen Jo, you know? She's a much better proposition.'

How would she take it when she realised the dog

had chosen *him* as his new owner? He suspected some part of her had already realised, but…

He folded his arms across his knees and rested his chin on them. She'd take it as more proof that she wasn't good enough, that she'd been overlooked once again.

He lifted his head and glared at the glorious breakers rolling in. Why on earth couldn't she see how gorgeous she was? She'd mentioned something about her grandmother and great-aunt having a challenging relationship. Did that extend to her as well? Did they make her feel she hadn't measured up? A scowl lowered through him. Or had some jerk made her doubt her own loveliness?

So what if she wasn't one of those little stick figures who paraded around in tiny dresses and squealed that a carrot stick would make them gain weight? It was no fun cooking for those women. It would be fun to cook for Jo, though.

If he still cooked.

He blew out a breath. If he'd met Jo before all this had happened…

But he hadn't.

He clenched a handful of sand in his fist before releasing it. He couldn't imagine going through his entire life believing he was completely unattractive to the opposite sex.

He'd been lucky. Until the accident. Now he could definitely relate. No woman would look twice at him—

He froze.

Jo had. In fact Jo had kissed him with so much unbridled hunger and joy that… Well, it meant he'd been mistaken. There was at least one beautiful woman who found him desirable enough to kiss. He scowled. Even if she had discounted the possibility of something deeper and more permanent with him.

You discounted it first.

He swallowed. He'd kissed her and she'd given him an unexpected gift. She'd made him realise that other people might see beyond his scars too.

Which was a moot point if he never left this place. But if he ever did manage to pay off his debts? Well, it would matter then. Either way, it had lightened something inside him.

Could he make her realise she was beautiful too?

How? Not by kissing her, that was for sure. That would lead to too much trouble and too much heartbreak. Until he could guarantee Ethan would be looked after for the rest of his life Mac wasn't free to offer any woman his heart.

But it didn't stop him from liking the way she looked. He loved her height, her stature, and the way she held herself. She was strong and powerful—a force to be reckoned with. And she'd fitted into his arms as if she'd been designed to be there.

He turned to Bandit. 'How can I prove to her that she's gorgeous?'

Bandit merely rolled onto his back, presenting his belly for a rub. Mac stared. 'Bandit! You're not a boy dog!' He ran his hand over the fur of Bandit's tummy. 'You're a girl dog.'

He ran both hands gently over Bandit's tummy and started to laugh.

'You're a girl dog who I *think* is expecting puppies.'

CHAPTER SIX

MAC FOUND JO in the kitchen and opened his mouth to give her the news about Bandit, eager to get things on an easy footing between them again and hoping this latest news would push the memory of their kiss—kisses—to the nether regions of their minds, where it would never see the light of day again.

Jo beat him to the punch, though. 'You had a phone call,' she said, without preamble.

She didn't smile, and his nape and his top lip both prickled with sudden perspiration. There was only one person who called the house phone. Russ and his friends had his mobile number, though they usually resorted to email.

'Mrs Devlin,' she said—unnecessarily, though she couldn't know that.

'How...?' He swallowed. 'How's Ethan doing?'

'She didn't say.'

A weight settled across his shoulders. He pulled out the nearest chair and fell into it. 'Did she want me to ring her back?' Which was a ridiculous question. Of course she'd want him to return her call.

'She didn't say.'

He stared at her and she finally turned from where she was rinsing a few dishes and shrugged.

'She hung up on me.'

He closed his eyes. He could imagine the conclusion Diana Devlin had come to upon hearing a woman's voice at the end of his phone—especially a voice as rich and honeyed as Jo's.

When he opened his eyes he found a glass of water sitting in front of him. He drained it.

'She's a cheery soul, isn't she?'

'Jo, she's spent the last few months in fear for her son's life and now she fears for his future. There isn't much in her life to feel cheerful about.'

'Garbage.' She dried a plate. 'Her son's alive, isn't he? That's something to be grateful for. His recovery is coming along nicely, isn't it? Another thing to be grateful for.'

'He'll bear the scars from this accident for the rest of his life.'

'Oh, for heaven's sake—we're not going to have this argument again. Ethan's mother will love him no matter what he looks like.'

She bent down to place the plate in a cupboard

and Mac got an eyeful of the curve of her hips. His heart started to pound. Jo had the kind of hips that could make a man salivate. He dragged his gaze to the glass he twirled between his fingers. He lifted it to his lips and managed to find another drop or two, but they did nothing to ease the thirst coursing through him.

Jo turned around. He kept his gaze on the glass.

'All I can say,' she said, 'is that I wouldn't want her in *my* sick room.'

Slowly he lifted his head to stare at her. She squeezed out the dishcloth and wiped down the table, not meeting his eyes. As far as he could tell the table was perfectly clean as it was, but he lifted both the glass and his arms out of her way and did his best not to draw the scent of her into his lungs.

'She's his mum. She'll be his best source of support...' He trailed off. He hadn't thought about it before. Not in that context. Ethan *was* doing okay, wasn't he?

For the first time he wished he hadn't so comprehensively cut himself off from his colleagues on the show.

He rose. 'I'll...um...' For heaven's sake—he didn't have to justify his every movement to her.

Turning on his heel, he strode out of the kitchen

and headed upstairs. Seizing his mobile from the desk he punched in Mrs Devlin's number. As he waited for her to answer he glanced at the curtains. He moved to close them, to shut out the day, and then stopped. He didn't have the heart for it. What difference would a bit of sunlight make? Even if Mrs Devlin cared, she'd never have to know.

'Malcolm,' she said, obviously having checked her caller ID before answering. She never called him Mac. She never said hello. She just said Malcolm.

'How are you, Mrs Devlin?'

She didn't answer him. She usually made some sarcastic comment—*How did he think she was, sitting at her son's sick bed day in day out?*

While he welcomed the silence he forced himself to push on. 'I understand you rang earlier?'

He waited for her to demand to know who Jo was and what she was doing in his house. He could imagine her sarcasm when he told her Jo was his temporary housekeeper. It would be something along the lines of *It's nice for some.*

'I wanted to tell you that this quarter's bills have come in.'

He closed his eyes. This lot would just about clean him out. To receive a much-needed portion of his advance he had to get something substantial to his publisher. *Soon.* That would cover the next quarter's costs. After that… He swallowed. If necessary he'd sell the car, his Sydney apartment. And then this house.

And if Ethan's treatment needed to continue after that… He rested his forehead against the glass sliding door, welcoming its coolness against his skin. They'd better hope this cookbook did well. *Really* well.

'Malcolm?'

It hit him that her voice lacked its usual stridence, though it could by no means be considered friendly.

'Please send the bills to my lawyer. I'll take care of them.' His heart pounded. 'How's Ethan?'

'He's doing as well as can be expected.'

It was her standard line whenever he asked. And he always asked. He didn't ask her to send his best to the younger man. She'd made it clear that Ethan wanted nothing to do with him.

'How…?' She cleared her throat. 'How are *you*?'

He nearly dropped the phone. He coughed and swallowed back his automatic reply—*fine*. That would seem a mockery, considering Ethan's condition. 'I…I'm working hard at wrestling this cookbook into shape.' She knew he meant all its profits to go to Ethan.

'Right. Goodbye, Malcolm.'

'Uh…goodbye.'

He stared at the phone. Normally she hung up without so much as a by-your-leave. What on earth was going on?

He threw the phone back to the desk and dragged a hand through his hair. Was everything really okay with Ethan? Had he suffered some setback? He paced across the room. Could Diana have said something to Jo? Who knew? Maybe they'd had a moment of woman-to-woman bonding. Maybe—

'She's a cheery soul, isn't she?'

Hell.

He clattered back down the stairs. Jo wasn't in the kitchen. She wasn't in the living or dining rooms either, but as he walked through the house he couldn't help noticing how light and airy it all seemed. The curtains were pulled back and sunlight poured in at freshly cleaned windows. The heavy wooden furniture gleamed, the rugs were plush underfoot, and plump scatter cushions invited him to recline on the sofa. Not that he spent any time in this part of the house any more.

Why not?

He ground his teeth together. His life consisted of eat, sleep and work. It didn't leave room for loafing on the sofa in front of the television.

He pushed out to the veranda and strode halfway down the steps to survey the view in front of him. But there was no sign of a tall, lush woman striding down that field of native grass, or along the beach with Bandit. Maybe she was pegging laundry on the line. He turned back.

'Are you looking for me?'

He started at the voice to his left and found Jo on her knees, pulling weeds from a garden bed. He was pretty sure that wasn't part of her job description.

He nodded towards the few spindly rose bushes. 'I'm not sure you need to worry about those.'

'I want to.'

Whatever... He planted his legs. 'What did you say to Mrs Devlin?'

'Ah.' She went back to digging. 'I told her to wake up to herself.'

He choked. 'You *what*?' He dropped to the bottom step, head in hands. 'Hell, Jo, the poor woman has been worried half out of her wits and—'

'I said it in a nice way.'

He lifted his head.

'I didn't say the actual words, *Wake up to yourself.*'

That had been her message, though.

'She had a big go at me for being here. I didn't like her insinuation, so I set her straight.'

He opened his mouth. After a moment he shut it again. He deserved everything Diana threw at him, but Jo didn't. She'd had every right to defend herself, to demand respect.

'When she started mouthing off that you didn't deserve the luxury of a housekeeper I…' She shrugged.

'You what?'

'I told her you were working so hard you were in danger of falling ill. And I made it clear that if that happened you wouldn't be able to earn. And that, therefore, her cash cow would dry up.'

'Tell me you put it nicer than that?'

'I expect I did.' She dusted off her hands and rested back on her heels. 'Like you, she's been focussing on all the wrong things.'

His mouth dried. What else had Jo said to the poor woman?

'I told her she needed to choose between her desire for revenge on you and what was best for her son.'

He clenched his jaw so hard he thought he might crack a tooth. 'I wish you'd kept your mouth shut.'

She rose and planted her hands on her hips, towering over him. Her chest rose and fell, her eyes flashed, but even when she was angry her voice washed over him like a balm.

'She's turned you into her whipping boy. What's worse is that you've let her.'

He shot to his feet. 'I owe that family!'

'Codswallop!' She glared. 'Next you're going to tell me you're responsible for the national debt and world hunger.'

'Don't be ridiculous.'

'What did you do that was so bad, huh? You yelled at an apprentice. Even if it hadn't been scripted, we've all been hauled over the coals by our bosses before. In the view of things that you're taking one could equally accuse Ethan of being a spineless little ninny. I mean *he's* the clumsy clod who dropped a tray of cold food into hot oil.'

He couldn't believe what he was hearing.

'I'm yelling at you now, but if you trip up the stairs in a huff and sprain an ankle is that going to be *my* fault? I don't think so, buster.'

'That's different. We're equals!' he hollered back. 'On set I had seniority, and that boy—'

'Oh, and that's another thing that's getting up my nose. You keep referring to Ethan as a boy—but he's nineteen years old. He's a man. He has the right to vote and he has the right to choose what kind of work he wants to do. He *chose* to work with you. He *wanted* to be a part of your team. You wanted your show to be a success, and you've been blaming your ambition for the accident. You forget that Ethan wanted the show to be a success too—why else was he there?—but you don't take *his* ambition into account.'

His mind whirled at her words, but he lifted his chin and set his shoulders. None of that made a scrap of difference.

'No,' she carried on, 'you won't take *any* of that into account, will you? It's much easier to carry on the way you have been.'

Something inside him snapped. 'Easier!' He started to shake with the force of his anger. 'Tell me how any of this is easy?' he yelled. 'Every day—*every single day*—I have to fight the urge to go driving in my glorious car, resist the impulse to go down to the beach and relish the feel of salt water against my skin, turn my back on the desire to race into the kitchen and try out a new recipe that's exploded into my mind!'

With each named temptation he flung his arm out as he paced up and down in front of the garden bed.

'I chain myself to my computer all day to write a book I should be qualified and competent to write. But instead I find myself battling with it as if it's an enemy that's determined to bring me down. So will you kindly tell me how any of that is *easy*?'

She moved to stand in front of him. She stood on a slightly higher piece of ground than he did so she was almost eye to eye with him.

'It's easier than facing the consequences of the accident.'

Ice crept across his scalp.

'It's easier than attempting to rebuild your life.'

He didn't have a life, and for as long as Ethan remained in hospital he didn't deserve a life.

She gave a mirthless laugh, as if she'd read that thought in his face. 'You really feel *that* responsible for Ethan?'

That wasn't worth dignifying with an answer.

'Then this—' she gestured all around '—is easier than meeting with Ethan face to face, easier than witnessing his struggles, and easier then offering him the true moral support of a friend.'

He had to swallow before he could speak, and

he felt every last drop of anger draining away. 'I have it on good authority that the last thing Ethan wants is to clap eyes on me.'

'Ethan's mother is *not* a good authority—and if you think she is then you're an idiot.'

He couldn't speak past the lump that had stretched his throat into a painful ache.

'Have you even spoken to Ethan yourself?'

He hadn't. Diana had demanded that he not plague her son, that Mac leave Ethan in peace. Call him a coward, but he hadn't *wanted* to speak to Ethan—hadn't wanted to hear the boy's recriminations.

'A real man would show up and say sorry.'

It was Russ's voice that sounded in his head now. He shied away from the thought, from what it demanded of him. What good would facing Ethan do for either one of them? He would do whatever he could not to upset the younger man. But he *could* check up on him—see how he was doing. He could ring Terry, the creative director, or one of the producers of the show. He'd bet someone from the old team would know.

He could at least ring. Not Ethan, but one of the others. How hard could that be?

'I do have one final burning question.'

He blinked himself back into the here and now to find Jo halfway up the steps to the house.

'Precisely what calamity do you think will befall us—' she shot the words over her shoulder '—if you *did* go for a drive in your car, or went for a swim, or if you *did* go and cook some delicious meal?'

She didn't wait for an answer but continued straight into the house on those long, strong legs of hers.

'So that was a hypothetical question, then?' he muttered.

Good. Because he didn't have an answer for it.

Jo sensed the exact moment when Mac loomed in the dining room's doorway. She didn't turn from where she'd set down dishes of new potatoes and buttered green beans.

'You're just in time. Take a seat.'

'On one condition.'

She turned at that. 'What?'

'That we call a truce and promise not to holler at each other for the next hour.'

The tension in her shoulders melted away. 'Make it two and you have yourself a deal.'

His lips lifted. Not quite a smile, but almost. Maybe they'd achieve one by the end of the meal.

He took a seat. 'Did you have any trouble with my instructions?'

'I don't think so. Proof is in the pudding, though, so to speak.'

She went to retrieve their steaks, oddly nervous as she set his plate in front of him.

He helped himself to potatoes and beans. Jo dug straight into her steak, slathered in béarnaise sauce. She closed her eyes. *Oh, dear Lord, the sauce was to die for.* She'd be lining up for his cookbook the moment it came out.

'You've overcooked your steak.'

She opened her eyes. 'Try yours.'

He did.

'And?' she prompted.

'It's perfect.'

'For you, maybe.' She wrinkled her nose. 'I prefer my steak properly cooked—not underdone, the way you seem to like it.'

'This is *not* underdone. It's how steak should be cooked.'

'And the sauce?'

He frowned. 'You've cooked it a little too long and it's started to separate.'

Truly? She stared at it.

'It's a pity about the tarragon vinegar, and you used too much onion to flavour the reduction, but only an experienced foodie would know.'

He frowned at her steak again, but she ignored the silent censure. 'Relax, Mac.' She reached for the beans. 'I'm actually pretty chuffed with my efforts—and that's the point, isn't it?'

He blinked.

'I mean the people who try out your recipes—they're going to adjust them to their own tastes, right? Like I did with my steak?'

'I guess.'

'But as long as they feel they've created a nice meal they're going to be happy, aren't they? Mission accomplished.'

He straightened as if she'd zapped him. 'You're right. Nobody's going to be assessing their creations with a mark out of ten.'

'Uh, no.'

She tried not to focus on the shape of his lips, or the scent of coconut that came from his still-damp hair. Hair that was a touch too long. Hair that had felt glorious when she'd run her fingers through it and—

She reached for her glass of water and drained it.

'I think I've been getting too hooked up on every detail.'

He really did need to let up a bit.

'But as long as my targeted audience is satisfied then that's the best I can hope for.'

Yup.

He suddenly grinned. Her heart skidded, and then settled to pound too hard too fast. She took back her earlier wish that he'd smile. She wished he wouldn't. Why couldn't her heart just behave normally around him?

'So, have you come any closer to discovering your new career path today?'

This had become a habit—at dinnertime he'd throw suggestions at her about a new vocation.

'Go on—thrill me,' she said. *Not literally.*

'Chef?'

She wrinkled her nose. 'I expect I'd need to like cooking for that.'

'You don't like to cook?'

'I never became interested in it until I started watching your show. Russ made all of us watch it.' She blew out a breath. 'But I'm afraid you're not going to make a convert of me. It's all far too fiddly for my liking.'

'Gardener, then?'

'It's a pleasant enough way to while away an hour or two, but a whole day of it? A whole week of it? Month after month? No, thanks.'

Bandit pattered into the dining room. 'Then maybe you'd like a stint as a dog breeder?' Mac's grin suddenly widened. 'It could be the perfect fit. I discovered today that Bandit is, in fact, Bandita.'

'What?'

'He is a she. Bandit is a girl dog.'

Her jaw dropped. 'You're joking?'

'I take it you didn't check before you agreed to adopt him…uh…her?'

She stared at the dog. 'It never occurred to me to check. I mean he's…she's…fluffy, and has lots of fur, and it's not like it's…um…obvious. I just—'

She folded her arms and glared. 'That nice old man told me Bandit was a boy.'

'I suspect "that nice old man" has taken you for a ride.'

'Why, though? What's the big deal if Bandit is a boy or a girl? It certainly makes no difference to me, and—'

She broke off at his laughter. He looked so different when he laughed.

She moistened her lips. 'What?'

'Bandit is a girl dog who I suspect is going to be a mother in the not too distant future.'

'Noooo...'

'Yes.'

'So that nice old man was just trying to fob Bandit off onto some poor sucker?'

'Bingo.'

And she was the sucker.

She stared at Bandit. She stared at Mac. 'We're going to have puppies?'

'Looks that way.'

Puppies? She grinned. She ate some more steak. 'Well, that'll be fun.' In the next instant she stiffened. 'What else did that rotten old man lie about? Is she microchipped? Has she had her vaccinations?' She set her knife and fork down. 'Well, that's that, then.'

Mac frowned. 'That's what?'

'It means I'll have to take her to the vet's tomorrow for a thorough check-up.'

'It wouldn't hurt,' he agreed.

She found herself grinning again. 'Puppies, huh? Do you think there's any money in dog breeding?'

'Not really.'

Oh, well. She'd think of something on the job front soon enough.

She gestured to the food. 'I don't think this effort has disgraced me.'

'Absolutely not.'

But he didn't meet her eye as he said it. Her heart started to thump. There was loads of time yet to learn all she needed to know about *macaron* towers.

She swallowed. Béarnaise sauce one day. *Macarons* the next.

'What on earth are you trying to do?'

Jo turned at Mac's voice. Bandit twisted out of her grasp and ran a few paces away, where she turned to glare at Jo. Jo let a growl loose from her throat. 'I'm trying to get Bandit into The Beast.' She gestured to her car. 'But Bandit doesn't seem too enamoured with the idea of going for a ride. Either that or it's the V-word—V. E. T.—that has her spooked.'

She pushed her hair off her face, thinking she must look a sight before telling herself that it didn't matter one iota what she looked like.

'For heaven's sake, how hard can it be? I'm bigger than her. I'm stronger than her. And if you make one derogatory comment about my intelligence in comparison to hers you'll be getting fish fingers for dinner.'

He raised his hands. 'No comments, derogatory or otherwise. I'm hoping for a cheese soufflé. I just put the recipe on the kitchen counter.'

She hoped it would taste as good as the words sounded coming from his lips. 'Do I need to pick up any exotic ingredients?'

'Not for today—but you'll need these for later in the week.'

He handed her a shopping list. Wrapped inside it was some housekeeping money.

'Here, Bandit.' He clicked his fingers and Bandit was at his side in an instant.

Jo scowled. Typical female. She rolled her shoulders. Actually, when she thought about it, she couldn't fault Bandit's taste.

'Up.' He patted the front passenger seat and Bandit leapt up and settled there. Mac turned back to Jo. 'There you go. I'll see you when you get back.'

He started to walk away and Bandit immediately leapt down to follow him.

'Ahem…'

Mac turned at Jo's cleared throat. He shook his head. 'C'mon, Bandit, let's try that again.'

This time when Bandit was seated in the car Mac

shut the door. But when he started to walk away Bandit set up a long, mournful howl.

'Don't cry, lovely girl.' Jo reached into the window to pat her. 'It's okay.'

None of which made the slightest difference. Bandit continued to howl.

Jo swung back to Mac. 'She's pregnant. I'm pretty sure that means she's not supposed to get upset.'

He lifted both arms. 'What do you want me to do about it?'

'It's more than obvious what needs to happen.'

'What's that?'

'You're going to have to come with us.'

Mac's face shuttered. 'That's out of the question.'

Jo took one look at him and had to rest her hands on her knees for several long moments. Pulling in a breath that helped haul her upright, she opened the car door to release Bandit—who leapt down in an instant.'

'I'm sorry, beautiful girl.' She went to fondle Bandit's ears, but the dog dodged away from her and for some reason it cut her to the quick. It was all she could do not to cry.

'What are you doing?'

Disbelief was etched across every line of Mac's

face. A face, it occurred to her now, that had become a little too familiar to her.

She tried to swallow the lump in her throat, but only partially succeeded. 'I'm not going to put her through that kind of distress. Not while she's in such a delicate condition.' Her voice came out high and tight, due to the lump. 'She'll hurt herself, or spontaneously abort. Or…' She shook her head, her stomach churning. 'I'm not going to be responsible for that.'

She walked past Mac and tried to hold her head up high.

'But… But…' he spluttered.

She stopped and waited, but he didn't say any more. She turned. 'Are you waiting for me to bully you? If you are you'll be waiting a long time. You're an adult. You know what's right and wrong.'

His jaw went tight and a tic started up beneath his right eye.

'I'm going to conserve my energy for when I have to contend with Bandit *and* her puppies when I eventually leave.' That was going to be awfully traumatic for poor Bandit. The thought made her stomach churn even harder.

'You can't take her when you leave.'

Jo started to stalk away, but he strode after her.

'She loves it here. Jo, I… Look, I know it's unfair, but she's adopted *me*—bonded with *me*. I didn't mean for it to happen.'

From the corner of her eye she saw the weak excuse for a smile that he shot her.

'I'll make a deal with you. You keep the puppies and Bandit stays here with me. I'll look after her—I promise.'

'Look after her?' She whirled to face him. 'You can't even take her to the vet! I can't in any conscience leave her here—even though she loves you and merely tolerates me. Even though I know she'll be way happier here than she will be with me.'

He took a step back from her, his mouth pressed so tight it turned his lips white.

'I don't know why I expected something better from you. You wouldn't even visit your brother when he was in hospital, though you had to know it was the thing he most wanted.'

He'd frozen to stone.

There was no room in his life for compassion or love or responsibility to his family…just a manufactured guilt that took over his every breathing moment.

She turned away, not knowing why her heart hurt so hard.

CHAPTER SEVEN

JO COUNTED OUT the eggs she'd need for the soufflé and had started to read the 'Hints on soufflés' section of a cooking website she'd found when voices floated in through the open front door.

Voices? She lifted her head and frowned. Surely not? She hadn't heard *voices*—as in more than one person speaking, having a conversation—since she'd arrived. She didn't count the way either she or Mac spoke to Bandit. Or her and Mac's often fraught and adversarial conversations.

He doesn't kiss like an adversary.

He kissed like a dream.

Stop it!

She cocked her head and listened harder. There was definitely more than one voice.

The voices grew stronger as she marched through the house. She pulled up short of the front door when she found Mac talking to an unknown man by the front steps—a man carrying what looked like a doctor's bag.

Mac didn't appear the least bit self-conscious. Could the man be an old friend?

She looked at the bag again and then it hit her. A *vet*! Mac had called out a vet.

She had to fight the urge to race outside and throw her arms around him. Oh, he'd love that, wouldn't he? *Not.* She straightened her shirt and then pushed outside as if it what was happening in front of her was the most normal thing in the world.

Could Mac conquer his fear of what the world thought of him one person at a time? She crossed her fingers behind her back.

She strode across the veranda. 'I thought I heard voices.'

'Jo, this is Daniel Michener. He's the local mobile vet.'

She hadn't considered for a moment that this area would warrant a mobile vet.

'There are a lot of hobby farms—not to mention dairy farms—in the area,' Daniel explained when she said as much. 'It's a bit hard to bring a cow, horse or an alpaca into the surgery.'

Which made perfect sense when she thought about it. 'Well, I'm really glad you can give Bandit a once-over.'

'I understand you adopted her and know nothing of her history?'

Jo grimaced. 'I was told she was a purebred seven-year-old male border collie, microchipped, neutered, and fully vaccinated.'

He laughed. 'Let's take a look at her, then.'

Mac played veterinary nurse, soothing Bandit and convincing her to co-operate with Daniel. He made a rather nice veterinary nurse, with those big hands gentle on the dog's neck. She shivered at the way he'd run a hand down Bandit's back while talking to her in low, reassuring tones. The sight of the broad man with the small, fine-boned, not to mention *pregnant* dog made her heart pitter-patter.

He glanced up and caught her staring, raised an eyebrow. She shrugged and forced her gaze back to Bandit, tried to ignore the way her breath hitched in her chest.

The vet gave Bandit a clean bill of health. 'You should expect the puppies in about a month.' He clicked his bag shut. 'My best guess, looking at her teeth, is that she's three years old—and this is not her first litter, so she'll probably be a good mother.'

Not her first?

She moved in a little closer and Mac's scent—all

warm cotton, coconut and dog—hit her. It was all she could do not to swoon. She had to step back again.

'Can you tell how many puppies she's going to have?'

He shook his head. 'With a border collie, though, you can expect somewhere between four and eight.'

Eight!

The vet handed her his bill. Mac stood beside her as they waved him goodbye.

'Can Bandit stay here with me?' Mac said without preamble. 'I promise I'll look after her.'

'Yes.'

He plucked the bill from her fingers. 'She's my dog now, so I'll take care of her bills.' He strode back towards the house. 'But those puppies, Jo...' he called over his shoulder. 'They're all yours.'

Puppies? She smiled. *Eight* puppies? She groaned. What on earth would she do with eight puppies?

Maybe Russ would like one after he'd recovered from his surgery. Weren't pets supposed to be good for people—a form of therapy?

She bit back a sigh. What Russ really needed was a visit from his brother.

Mac ostensibly studied the cheese soufflé that Jo had set on the table, but all the time his mind whirled. Tomorrow Jo would have been here for a week. *What did she mean to tell Russ?*

He glanced at her. She wiped her hands down the sides of her jeans. 'Does it pass muster?'

He pulled his attention back to the soufflé. 'On first glance, yes. It's a nice colour.'

She folded her arms, narrowing her eyes.

'Okay, okay.' He raised his hands. 'I'd want it higher and fluffier if you were one of my apprentices—but you're not. This is the very first time you've made a soufflé, right?'

'Right.'

'Then in that case it definitely passes muster.'

She sat and motioned for him to serve it.

He drew the warm scent of the soufflé into his lungs. 'It smells good.'

She leaned in closer to smell it too, her lips pursed in luscious plumpness. A beat started up inside him, making his hand clench around the serving spoon.

'So this whole food-assessing thing...it's a bit like wine-tasting? You check the colour of the thing, smell it and finally taste it?'

'Though in this instance one hopes it doesn't get spat back out.'

She sort of smiled. There hadn't been too many smiles from her in the last day and a half.

What was she going to tell Russ?

'I'm trying to get away from the demanding level of perfection that's necessary in a top-notch restaurant. The people who buy my book aren't cooking for royalty.' Not like he had. They'd be cooking for their eighty-five-year-old grandmothers. 'I'm correct in thinking, aren't I, that they just want to have some fun?'

'Fun.' She nodded, but he could tell she held back a sigh.

He shook his head. How was he going to teach her the intricacies of a *macaron* when she didn't even like cooking?

He pushed the thought from his mind and sampled a forkful of soufflé.

'Well?'

He'd give it to her straight. Somehow she sensed it whenever he fudged. And she didn't seem to mind the criticism. *Because she wants to get better.* Yes, but he wasn't sure her reasons for wanting to get better were going to help her conquer the laborious process of making a *macaron* tower. He shook that thought away. If she left tomorrow there'd be no need to figure that out.

The thought of her leaving filled him with sudden darkness. He moistened his lips. He didn't want her leaving because he wanted her to tell Russ that there was nothing to worry about. That was all.

He dragged his mind back to the soufflé. 'An accomplished soufflé should be lighter. You probably needed to whip the egg whites a bit longer. But it's very good for a first effort.'

'You mean it's passable?'

He needed to work on that whole giving-it-to-her-straight thing.

She sampled it too, and shrugged. 'I don't understand the difference between beating, whipping, creaming, mixing and all that nonsense.'

It wasn't nonsense.

'What's all that about anyway?'

He stared at her. 'Would it help if I put a glossary defining those terms in the book?'

'Yes!' She pushed her hair off her face. 'I mean *I'd* welcome one.'

Done.

'And could you also add a definite length of time for how long egg whites should be whipped?'

'That depends on the size of the eggs, the temperature of the room in which you're whipping them, the humidity in the air and any number of other factors.'

She stared at him. He wished he could ignore the intriguing shape of her mouth. He wished he could forget their softness and the spark they'd fired to life inside him.

'Mac?'

He jumped. 'What?'

'I just asked if you could include a photo, then, of what properly beaten egg whites should look like?'

He wrote that down on the pad he'd started to keep at his elbow when they had dinner. With the addition of Jo's suggestions, the cookbook finally felt as if it were taking shape. He just had to re-member he wasn't writing a textbook for apprentices.

In the kitchen, the oven timer dinged. He frowned. 'What else are you cooking?'

She didn't answer. She was already halfway to the kitchen.

She returned with a pizza. One of those frozen jobs she'd shoved in the freezer after her first shopping trip. *What on earth...?*

She took one look at his face and laughed. 'I'm a carnivore, Mac. I'm sure cheese soufflé with a vegetable medley is all well and good, in its place, but give me a meat lovers' pizza every time.'

She seized a slice and proceeded to eat it with gusto. His stomach tightened, his groin expanded, and it was all he could do not to groan out loud.

She tilted her chin at the pizza. 'Help yourself.'

'I haven't eaten that pap since I was a teenager. It's full of chemicals and MSG and—'

'You don't know what you're missing.' She suddenly grinned, and it made him realise how remote and subdued she'd been. 'Have a slice and I'll put you out of your misery.'

His chin came up. 'What misery?'

'What I'm going to tell Russ tomorrow.'

He didn't try pretending that it didn't matter. It mattered a lot.

Without another word he took a slice of pizza and bit into it. 'Yuck, Jo!' He grimaced and she laughed. 'This is truly appalling.'

If she liked pizza that much he'd make her a pizza that would send her soul soaring—

He would if he still cooked, that was.

She reached for a second slice. 'On one level I know that. Whenever I eat pizza from a restaurant I can tell how much better it is. But this…? I don't know—I still like it.'

He finished his slice and gazed at what was left. 'It's strangely satisfying. Addictive.'

She was right. He reached for a second slice and polished it off. 'What *are* you going to tell Russ?'

He watched as she delicately licked her fingers— eight of them. He adjusted his jeans. He drained his glass of water. *Don't look. Don't think. Don't kiss her again.*

She rose and opened the bottle of red wine sitting on the sideboard. He hadn't noticed it before. He didn't know if she was making him wait to punish him, or whether she was trying to gather her thoughts.

She handed him a glass of wine and sat. 'I'm going to tell Russ that you're one of the most pigheaded, stubborn men I've ever met. I'm going to tell him you argue every point, and that whenever your work is interrupted you have creative type-A tantrums that would do a toddler proud. I'm going to tell him that you sulk and scowl and swear under your breath. And I'm going to tell him you've stolen my dog.'

He stared at her and the backs of his eyes prickled and burned. 'I could kiss you.'

Everything she'd just said was designed to allay

each and every one of Russ's fears. He couldn't have done better himself.

'I'm not going to tell him that.'

The air between them suddenly shimmered with a swirl of unspoken desires and emotions as the memory of the kiss they'd shared rose up between them. He knew she recalled it too, because her eyes dilated in exactly the same way as they had before he'd kissed her the last time.

And it had to be the last time. *Don't kiss her again!*

But the way her lips parted and her breathing became shallow…it could slay a man.

She dragged her gaze away and took a sip of wine, but even in the dim light he could see how colour slashed high on her cheekbones. He searched his mind for something to say.

'Do you really mind about Bandit?'

Her lips twisted. 'More than I should, I suspect. But not so much now I know there are puppies on the way.'

Her chin came up and her gaze lasered him to the spot.

'Can I ask you a question?'

He set his glass down. 'If I get to ask one of you in return.'

She twirled her glass in her fingers. Eventually she set her glass down too.

'Deal.'

He stiffened his shoulders, because he didn't expect her question would be an easy one. That was okay. Neither was his.

'Shoot.'

'Why won't you visit Russ?'

He tried to not let her words bow him. He should have known this was what she'd ask.

'It's funny…you don't seem a particularly vain man.'

He wasn't.

'But actions speak louder than words.'

What was she talking about?

'Are you really *that* afraid of showing your ugly mug to the outside world?'

At any other time he'd have laughed at the 'ugly mug'. He happened to know for a fact that she was rather partial to his particular 'ugly mug' no matter how much she tried to hide it. Except…

Was that what she really thought of him?

His shoulders slumped. 'I'm not vain, Jo.'

She gnawed at her bottom lip, but didn't say anything.

He dragged a hand down his face. 'I made a

promise to Mrs Devlin that I would lie low and stay out of the limelight until Ethan was out of hospital. Tabloid journalists would hound me like a dog if they knew I was in Sydney.'

She opened her mouth, but he continued before she could voice her protests.

'They'd find out—no matter how quiet I tried to keep it.'

'Why did you make such a promise?'

'Because the media brouhaha surrounding me and the accident was seriously upsetting for Ethan.'

'And you wanted to do what you could to make things easier for him.'

'At the time I'd have done anything either he or his mother asked of me.' He still would. He leaned towards her. 'Why don't you think what I'm doing for Ethan is good enough?'

She reached out and twirled the stem of her wine glass in her fingers. 'Is that your question?'

Dammit! 'No.'

She didn't say a word. Just sat there like the rotten sphinx, sipping her wine. She picked a piece of pepperoni from the pizza and popped it into her mouth.

He watched the action, suddenly ravenously hungry. Their gazes clashed and she stilled mid-chew.

For a moment she was all that filled his vision, and then she looked away.

'What's your question?'

Her voice came out high and thready. He knew why. The same frustration coursed through his veins and made his skin itch. Would a brief physical relationship really be such a bad idea?

He forced himself back in his seat, closed his eyes and drew a deliberate breath into his lungs. He opened his eyes, but the question on his tongue about the relationship between her, her grandmother and her great-aunt dissolved, to be replaced by an altogether different one.

He leaned towards her and her eyes widened at whatever she saw in his face. 'What I want to know, Jo, is why you're so convinced that you're not beautiful? Who or what made you feel that way?'

She glanced away, traced the edge of her placemat. She opened her mouth, but he cut her off.

'I want the truth.' Not the lie he could see forming on her lips. 'If you won't give me the truth then don't give me anything.'

She swallowed and met his gaze. He stared back. He knew how forbidding he must look, but he wanted her to know he was serious about this.

'We might not be able to explore the physical relationship I'm aching to explore with you, but out here in the boondocks we can at least be honest with each other.'

Eventually she nodded. 'Okay.'

She pushed her hair behind her ears and then drained what was left of her wine—which was a not inconsiderable half-glass.

'When I was in school I was always teased for being a giant. I might have been picked first for basketball games, but I was always picked last at school dances. Boys obviously didn't like to date girls who were taller than them.'

He grimaced. Kids could be cruel.

'But when I was nineteen and at university I fell madly in love with a chemistry student. I thought…I thought he had feelings for me.' Her knuckles turned white around her glass. 'It turned out, though, that I was a bet—a dare. It was some kind of Chemistry Club challenge—the guy with the ugliest date for the Christmas party won.'

Mac couldn't believe what he was hearing. 'He… You—'

He broke off, shaking all over.

'Me and some of the other girls caught wind of it and dumped them all before the event, but…'

But it had made her doubt her beauty. And she'd been doubting it ever since.

She refilled their glasses and handed him one, glancing up at him from beneath her fringe, her eyes bruised and wounded.

'I don't want to talk about this, Mac. I answered your question and the conversation is now over.'

'No!' He exploded out of his chair. 'I can't believe you've let a bunch of immature jerks let you feel like this—made you feel ugly and worthless. You're beautiful and you're worth a million of them.'

'Go and see Russ, Mac, and then we can talk about this as much as you like. But until then— zip it.'

She rose, collected their plates and strode into the kitchen. He wanted to go after her, shake her and tell her those boys had been wrong. He curled a hand around the doorframe of the dining room before he could storm through it. If he went after her he'd kiss her. And this time neither one of them would stop.

He strode out to the front veranda, Bandit at his heels, into the chill night. If only he could get his hands on those cruel twerps. If only he could prove to her that she was beautiful.

You can. Go see Russ. For her.

He sat on the top step and held his head in his hands. That would mean something to her. But…

Go see Russ? Though he wanted to, with everything that was inside him, he couldn't break his promise.

Jo searched for signs of pity in Mac's face the next day, when he gave her a brand-new recipe to try out—coq au vin—but couldn't see any.

What did disconcert her was the way his gaze rested on her lips and the answering hunger that rose through her. She didn't want to want this man. She wished she hadn't told him that nasty sordid tale last night. She wished she'd been able to resist his appeal for honesty. He made her feel far too vulnerable.

She gazed at the recipe and gave her brain a metaphorical kick. *Think of something halfway intelligent to say.*

'So, this needs to simmer for a long time?'

'That's right.'

'Simmer, boil, poach, stew—all that nonsense should probably go in your glossary of terms.'

He wrote that down on his notepad. 'A genuine simmer is just below boiling point, but where there's still the occasional bubble surfacing.'

Right. She filed the information away.

'C'mon—sit down,' he ordered, gesturing to the kitchen table. 'There's hours before you need to get the stew on to simmer.'

'There's a lot of chopping to do,' she said, referring to the recipe.

He switched on the laptop he'd brought downstairs with him. 'Jo, not even *you* need five hours to chop some chicken and vegetables.'

He had a point. If only she hadn't done the grocery shopping yesterday afternoon she could have used that as an excuse to avoid him now. She sat, but she'd have much sooner grabbed the broom and started sweeping the laundry, or headed outside for a spot of weeding.

Anything except being in the same room as him, sitting so close to him. And if he thought they were going to continue last night's conversation then he was going to be sadly disappointed.

'What do you want?'

He raised an eyebrow and she knew she wasn't being particularly gracious—but then she didn't *feel* particularly gracious. She felt grumpy, out of sorts, frustrated...

She stuck her nose in the air. 'I'll have you know I'm very busy with important housemaidy things.'

His lips twitched. 'Do you think you can fit the making of tea into all that important housemaid business?'

With an exaggerated sigh, she rose and made tea while he fiddled around with his computer.

When she set the pot and two mugs on the table and took her seat again he said, 'We're going to take a vocational test.'

Something inside her started to shrivel. The sooner she worked out the next stage of her life the sooner she'd leave him in peace, right?

He fixed her with the clear blue of his eyes. 'You've helped me and now I want to help you.'

The shrivelling promptly stopped. He *wasn't* trying to get rid of her?

'Ready?'

She shrugged. 'I guess.'

He turned to the laptop. '"Are you more motivated by achievement or appreciation?"' he read.

She blinked. 'Um…' She liked to *see* the results of her hard work—as in the way Mac's house now currently shone after all her dusting and sweeping. 'Achievement.'

He leaned back in his chair with a frown. 'Are you sure?'

She glared back at him. 'Of course I'm sure.'

'Why do you want to make that *macaron* tower for your grandmother, then? Aren't you hoping to gain her appreciation and help her win a bet?'

What she really wanted to do was bring her grandmother and great-aunt's differences to an end. She knew they loved each other, so why couldn't they show it?

Because of her? She'd always been a bone of contention between them.

'Jo?'

She shook herself. 'Fine—whatever. Appreciation, then.'

His glare deepened. 'You have to take this seriously.'

She lifted her hands. 'I am.'

He glared at her for a few more seconds before returning to his computer. '"Do you tend to rely on your past experiences or on hunches?"'

She was tempted to fish a coin from her purse and toss it. 'Hunches...'

He checked the appropriate box just as she was about to change her answer. *Oh, well.*

'"Are you more interested in what is real or what is meaningful?"'

He stared at her. She stared back.

'Meaningful,' they said at the same time.

He asked her over sixty questions!

At the end he gave her a score. 'And that means… Hey!' he said when she took the computer from him.

She shook her head. 'Now it's your turn.' Let's see how he liked being put under the microscope. '"Do you tend to be easily distracted or able to concentrate well?"'

He glared. 'I can concentrate just fine when I want to.'

She checked the box for 'easily distracted'. As far as she could tell Mac actively *searched* for distraction.

'"In most situations do you rely more on careful planning or improvisation?"'

He dragged a hand down his face. 'Improvisation—more's the pity. Or these recipes I'm trying to drag out of my head would be a lot easier to commit to paper.'

'"Do you prefer step-by-step instructions or to figure things out for yourself?"'

He scowled. 'If only I *did* prefer step-by-step instructions!'

She was going to have to get him cooking again. Somehow.

When they'd finished she gave him a score and then read out the associated job suggestions. '"Artist",' she said. Chef fitted into that category perfectly. '"Teacher. Entertainer."'

'Very funny.' He retrieved the computer.

She wasn't trying to be funny, but she kept her mouth shut.

'According to your score, you'd make a good girl scout. What *is* this garbage?'

'You tell me.'

'No, no—here we go. It says you'd be a good scientist.'

'Except I'm tired of being a scientist, remember?'

'You're tired of being a *geologist*,' hc corrected. 'You could go back to university and major in a different science.'

'Yay,' she said, with a deplorable lack of enthusiasm. 'Also, I want to live in a city. Find me a job in one of those.'

'Why?'

'I want to go to the cinema, and the library, and to big shopping centres and all those lovely things.'

All the places she'd missed when working in the Outback.

'Here we go. As you're apparently service-orientated you'd also make a good nurse.'

The sight of blood didn't worry her. But... 'I hate hospitals.'

He took on a sick pallor. 'Me too.'

And just like that she wanted to reach out and take his hand, offer silent support and comfort. He wouldn't welcome it. He'd probably kiss her in retaliation.

Ooh!

She pulled her hands into her lap. 'Well, that's certainly provided me with food for thought.'

'It was complete and utter nonsense!'

She smiled at him. 'I appreciate the effort.'

Finally—*finally*—he smiled back.

CHAPTER EIGHT

JO PULLED THE *macarons* from the oven and set the tray on a trivet. Hands on hips, she surveyed them. These weren't pretty, like the picture on the internet. They were crooked, misshapen and kind of flat. For the love of everything green and good! How hard could it be to make these fussy little confections?

She hunched over her laptop and reread the recipe, but she couldn't find where she'd gone wrong.

She'd made a halfway decent cheese soufflé. As far as she could tell her coq au vin had been good, even if Mac hadn't eaten very much of it. And, okay, so her béarnaise sauce hadn't held together the way it was apparently supposed to, but it had tasted just fine to her.

Her hands clenched. For a week now she'd been religiously following Mac's instructions and cooking recipes with names she couldn't even pronounce. She'd figured she was ready to try her hand at *macarons*.

She cast a glance at the tray and her lip curled. Apparently not.

Baring her teeth, she made a pot of tea and then pulled another egg carton towards her. She would master this if it was the last thing she ever did.

She separated eggs. She'd need to buy more. Luckily a nearby hobby farm sold farm-fresh eggs. The way she was going through the rotten things she'd be on a first-name basis with the owners of said hobby farm by the end of the week.

Mac strode into the kitchen, staring down at a sheet of paper in his hands. Tonight's recipe, she supposed. Yay, more cooking. She forgot all about cooking, though, when she noticed how amply he filled out his beaten-up jeans. The material stretched across strong thighs and she could almost see the muscles rippling beneath the denim.

He glanced up and froze when he saw what she was doing.

Her chin shot up. Well, bad luck, buddy! She'd been making his recipes for seven days now. *Seven days of cooking.*

He turned to leave. 'Don't even think about it.' Her voice came out on a snarl. He turned back and raised an eyebrow. 'Sit!' She pointed to a chair. She could see he was about to refuse. 'I will tie you to it if I have to.'

He blinked. His eyes turned dark and lazy. Deliberately his gaze lowered to her lips, all but caressing them. 'I'm almost tempted to put that to the test.'

She had to swallow. Wrestling with him would be so very intriguing.

And foolhardy.

She backed up one step and then another. She seized the tray of *macarons*. 'Look at these.'

He did, and then grimaced.

She dropped the tray to the table and swung away to pour him a mug of tea. She pushed it across the table towards him. 'Would you like a *macaron* to go with that?' she asked drily

His lips twitched, but he didn't sit. 'No, thanks.'

'Of course you don't. No rational person would touch one of those with a twenty-foot pole. Have you seen anything less appetising in your life?'

He took a hasty slug of his tea.

She glared. Why did this cooking gig have to be so *hard*? 'If you say one more thing against my béarnaise sauce I'll...'

'Tie me up?'

Images pounded at her. 'Pelt you with my *macarons*.'

He laughed. It seemed like an age since he'd laughed. 'A fate worse than death.'

She tilted her chin at the tray. 'Those suckers would probably knock you out. Please, Mac, I need your help. Can you please, please, *please* tell me what I did wrong?'

He sat and pulled the tray towards him and something inside her chest started to flutter and thrash. *Two birds. One stone.* If she could get him to do something that was halfway related to cooking it would teach her a technique she obviously needed and maybe—just maybe—it would help him overcome his resistance to preparing food again. Maybe he would find his way back to his passion and find some comfort in losing himself in it for a while.

'I suspect you didn't beat the egg whites for long enough.'

There seemed to be a theme emerging there.

'Or perhaps you didn't use enough confectioners' sugar. Or you cooked them at too high a temperature.'

There were too many variables. With a growl she finished separating the eggs—a full dozen—

and shoved the bowl and a whisk at him. 'Show me how it's done,' she demanded. 'There must be something wrong with my technique.'

His face closed up and his body drew in on itself, tight and unbending. 'You know I—'

'I'm ready to beg. And it's not real cooking, Mac. It's just whisking.'

And then it hit her—how she could keep him in the kitchen with her. She moistened her lips. 'I haven't really told you why it's so important that I master this stupid *macaron* tower, have I?'

'You mentioned the bet between your grand-mother and great-aunt.'

She snorted. 'Ah, the bet. It wasn't our finest hour I'm afraid. My grandmother had been flicking through a magazine and came across a picture of one and made some throwaway comment. I said it was pretty. Great-Aunt Edith then said there was no way on God's green earth—her words—that I could make one for my grandmother's next birthday. Grandma, thinking she was standing up for me, said I could do it standing on my head.'

He winced.

'Naturally, of course, I said it'd be a piece of cake.' *What an idiot.*

'And then the pearls were put up as a stake…?'

'It's like something from a bad comedy.' And she was caught squarely in the middle.

'Why did you let yourself get drawn in?'

'Habit. But lately I've been thinking it's a bad habit all round—this adversarial bent we've developed.'

'It must've been there before you came along.'

'I guess so, but I want to do something to change it. I want to mend it.'

He leaned in towards her and her heart did some more of that fluttering and thrashing.

'You know the whole "Russ having a heart attack and me suddenly re-evaluating my life" stuff. I know they love each other. So...'

'How are you going to change it?'

'I don't know yet.'

'Isn't making a *macaron* tower just falling in with their continued rivalry?'

She shrugged. 'My plan so far is that I make the best damn *macaron* tower that's ever been seen and then I take the pearls and claim them for my own.'

He started to laugh. 'I suspect that'd be something to see.' He sobered. 'But, Jo, isn't the necklace just the object of something that goes deeper between them?'

She slumped into a chair. 'I guess.'

'Tell me about them.'

So she did. She told him about Great-Aunt Edith first. 'I mean I know she loves me. And she's the one I most physically resemble. So it's odd—I can't understand why she's been on my case since, like, for*ever*. I shouldn't wear this and I shouldn't say that, and I shouldn't act like this and I shouldn't draw attention to myself like that, and I shouldn't wear my hair like this. On and on and on.'

It wore her out just thinking about it.

'It made me rebel in every dreadful way when I was a teenager. I wore tight pants and even tighter tops—things that didn't suit me. I'm afraid she was right on that subject.'

'And your grandmother?'

'My grandmother is the opposite. She's pretty, petite, and oh-so ladylike. She's stuck up for me forever, declaring I should wear, say and do whatever I damn well please—always telling me that I look gorgeous and pretty regardless of my get-up.' She glanced at Mac. 'And I'm afraid that's not always been the best advice to be given.'

It was her grandmother's vision that she'd never really been able to live up to.

He leaned back. 'They love each other, you say?'

'Oh, yes.' There wasn't a single doubt about that. 'But after one particularly vehement argument twelve months ago Great-Aunt Edith moved out.' Which was crazy. Her grandmother and aunt belonged together.

'Is it possible your great-aunt feels like you do—overshadowed by the petite women who surround her and made to feel she's never measured up?'

As far as Jo could tell, her great-aunt was indestructible.

Or was that just the attitude she assumed?

She sat up straighter.

'That attitude—it's wrong. You're a beautiful woman, Jo, which means your great-aunt must've been a great beauty too. But if she didn't believe herself beautiful, can you imagine how she must've felt, growing up with a sister who fitted into society's "classically beautiful" mould?'

Jo's throat tightened.

'If they love each other, as you say…'

'They do.' She might not be certain of much, but she was certain of that.

'Could it be that your grandmother is showing her love and acceptance for your great-aunt through you? If your great-aunt has felt overshadowed all these years then your grandmother treating you—

the child who looks so like her much-loved sister—with adoration and such disregard for what the world thinks... Well, that's powerful stuff.'

Wow.

Things started to fall into place.

Holy Cow! 'I don't know what to say.'

His eyes narrowed. 'You're not going to cry, are you?'

She tipped up her chin. 'Most certainly not.'

And that was when she noticed that he was whisking her egg whites. A fist tightened about her heart even as she noticed that his technique was way better than hers. *Keep it casual.*

'Wouldn't it be easier to use an electric beater?'

He glared and she raised her hands. 'Sorry—is that some weird food purist thing?'

Humour lit his eyes although it didn't touch his lips. 'It *would* be easier.'

'But?'

'But this kitchen doesn't happen to be stocked with that kind of equipment.'

Oh, that sealed it. She was going out and buying an electric mixer first thing tomorrow.

'Here—you try.'

She took the bowl and tried to mimic his whisking action.

He didn't grimace, but she suspected he wanted to. 'It just takes a bit of practice,' he assured her.

She wished she felt reassured.

'Oh, for heaven's sake, Jo!' he exploded a moment later. 'That whisk isn't a hammer. You're trying to whisk air into those egg whites.'

She held the bowl out to him. He didn't shrink back, but she could see what was going through his mind.

She snapped, 'This isn't *real* cooking. It's just some stupid egg whites and a rotten whisk.'

He ground his teeth together, snatching the bowl from her. 'You have an attitude problem when it comes to the kitchen.'

Wasn't that the truth?

'Look—*this* is how you're meant to be doing it.'

He demonstrated what he meant. He looked so at home with a whisk—kind of commanding and… right. She could watch him do this all day.

'Why did you grow up with your grandmother and great-aunt?'

She'd answer all the questions he wanted if he'd just keep whisking.

'There was a twenty-year age difference between my father and my mother. When I was five, my mother left. I think she was tired of hanging out with older people. When she left, Grandma and Great-Aunt Edith moved in.'

'Do you still see your mother?'

'Occasionally.' She peered into the bowl. 'She lives in the UK now. Aren't they done?'

'No. Test it.'

He kept hold of the bowl but handed her the whisk. She swirled it through the mixture.

'See?' he said. 'It's not thick enough yet.'

Right… She glanced at the tray on the table. Well, that was one question answered. She bounced up and measured out confectioners' sugar and set it on the table within Mac's easy reach.

'And your father?'

She wrinkled her nose. 'We're not close. He moved out to a bachelor pad when I was six. He's a geologist. I became a geologist because I thought it might give us something to talk about.'

'But?'

'But I don't like being a geologist—and if he has a problem with that then he can just suck it up.'

Mac stopped whisking to stare at her.

'Relationships are two-way streets. If he wants

a proper relationship with me then he needs to put in an effort too.'

'You sound kind of well-adjusted on that?'

She simply shrugged.

'Here—test the mixture now.'

She did.

'Feel how much stiffer it is? That's what you're aiming for.'

Oh, okay. So that explained the cheese soufflé too…

Mac looked ready to leave again. She handed the whisk back to him.

'My father is what he is. Grandma and Great-Aunt Edith have raised me, loved me and stood by me even when we've all been at loggerheads with each other. They're my family and they're important to me. I don't want to think what my childhood would've been like if it wasn't for them.'

'And that's why you want to bring their silly feuding over the pearls to an end? And you think a *macaron* tower will help?'

'It can't hurt.'

'Well, there's a start.' He pushed the bowl over to her. 'Perfectly whisked egg whites.'

He stood.

He couldn't leave yet! She took the sugar she'd

measured out earlier and went to tip the lot into the egg whites.

Mac's hand on her wrist stopped her. 'What are you doing?'

He sounded utterly scandalised.

She forced her eyes wide. 'I'm adding the sugar.'

'You're supposed to add it *slowly*.'

He proceeded to show her exactly how to add it, and how to beat it into the mixture. She might have feigned a bit more stupidity than necessary, but it was worth it to see him work. Surreptitiously she measured out the other ingredients and had them ready whenever he needed them.

She moistened her lips. *Keep telling him stories. Don't give him time to think about what he's doing.*

'Grandma and Great-Aunt Edith are the reason I want to move back to the city. They're eighty-five and eighty-three, respectively. I want to spend more time with them.'

He glanced up. 'So the cinemas, libraries, cafés—they're just…?'

'Attractive fringe benefits.'

He continued to stare at her. It took an effort not to fidget.

'They're getting on. They're independent, and in good health at the moment, but it won't last forever. When the time comes I want to care for them. They spent so much of their lives looking after me and…well, we're family and it matters.'

Russ's heart attack had taught her what the important things in life were and it wasn't a lesson she meant to forget.

Those blue eyes flashed and she swore she almost felt heat searing her skin.

'Are you trying to make me feel guilty about Russ?'

She blinked. 'Of course not.'

He pushed the bowl towards her and stood. 'I think you'll find your mix is ready.'

'Don't go, Mac. I'm not trying to make you feel bad about Russ. I tried that the other day and I'm not one to go back over old ground. I just wanted to make sure you knew how he felt—that while he won't say anything he's hurt that you haven't been to see him. Now that you do know the rest of it is up to you.'

'There is no "rest of it", Jo. There's nothing that can be done.'

'You could at least tell him why. You could at least acknowledge that you're letting him down and apologise. I understand you feel responsible for Ethan, but he's not the only person who needs you.'

This wasn't the way to make him stay.

She stuck out a hip. His gaze fixed on it for a heartbeat before returning to her face. She tried to control her breathing.

'Look, I'm doing my best with your rotten recipes, aren't I?'

'They're not supposed to be rotten.'

'Then why do I keep dreaming of fish-finger burgers?

He adjusted his stance. 'Your point being…?'

'I'm trying to help you out, so the least you can do is sit there and watch as I try to shape this unholy mess into pretty little *macarons*. Give me tips where appropriate and whatnot.'

He folded his arms, lowered his gaze to her hip again. When he raised it his eyes had started to gleam. 'I'll do it for a boon.'

A…*what*?

'A kiss.'

Something inside her softened. He smirked. She hardened it. Did he think she'd run away from the challenge? She hitched up her chin. She wasn't in any mood to be browbeaten.

'Done.'

A kiss on the cheek. She bit her inner cheek to stop from smiling. Simple.

'A kiss on the lips,' he said, as if he'd read her mind.

She could feel her eyes narrow. 'I thought you said kissing was a bad idea?'

'I was wrong. I want to kiss you. A lot. And for a long time. In fact I want to do more than kiss you, Jo.'

Everything inside her thrilled to his words. She should be running for the hills, but she needed steady legs for running and hers were far from steady. The temptation to follow the beat of this particular drum flooded through her. It addled her mind, but it didn't completely scramble it.

'Fine, then. A kiss on the lips. But no hands.' She didn't need even the tiniest bits of their bodies touching. 'And not until the *macarons* are in the oven.'

'Deal.'

He sat. Her heart chugged. This was craziness—absolute craziness. Why on earth did he want a kiss from a great lug like her?

'You're a beautiful woman.'

She didn't believe that for a moment, but she

couldn't deny the heat that flared between them. It didn't make sense, but it existed all the same.

She picked up a spoon.

'Your hands are shaking.'

She gritted her teeth and handed the spoon to him. 'Cooking makes me nervous. Show me how you dollop this mess out to make pretty little domes.'

'You don't *dollop* it. You pipe it.'

He flung open a kitchen drawer, seized a freezer bag and snipped off the end. She watched as he masterfully filled the makeshift piping bag and then proceeded to pipe a perfect row on her newly prepared cookie sheet.

'We'll take it in turns. You do the next row.'

His hands were steady. Hers weren't. That had to be the reason his rows looked so much neater than hers. And even while she lectured herself to pay attention and follow his instructions precisely all she could think about was what beautiful hands he had and what an idiot she'd been to make that no-hands rule for their kiss. It would be divine to have those fingers tracing across her naked flesh.

'They're ready to go in the oven now.'

Her pulse fluttered up into her throat, jamming her breath and making her knees tremble. *Don't show weakness.* She did what she could to force steel to her backbone. With an insouciance she was far from feeling she picked up the tray and moved towards the oven.

'Wait.'

She wanted to scream.

Mac clicked his tongue. 'I'd better check the oven temperature.'

It reminded her of what she'd just achieved in here. Mac had all but made those *macarons* himself.

He opened the oven door and put his hand inside. Apparently satisfied, he took the tray from her and placed it inside. When he turned back he wore the most satisfied smile she'd ever seen a male of the species wear.

'Now you have to kiss me.'

She might doubt her attractiveness to the opposite sex, but there was no denying the relish in Mac's grin. That relish gleamed from his eyes, practically spilling from his every pore. Her throat started to tighten. She couldn't trust it. Mac was a consummate actor.

She slammed her hands to her hips. 'You think it's fair to blackmail a kiss from me?'

'God, but you're beautiful when you flare up like that.'

The shrivelling started. 'And now I *know* you're not being serious. I've never been beautiful and—'

'I've never understood the urge some men have to bend a woman over their knee and give them six of the best…until now.'

Her eyes started from her head. Her throat thickened and she had to swallow a couple of times. 'You wouldn't dare!'

He leaned in close, his eyes blazing back into hers. 'You'd better think very carefully about what you say from here on. Believe me, Jo, you don't want to test me on this.' His lips hooked up with self-satisfaction. 'After all, you don't know what boon I might demand next time.'

She couldn't look away. 'What makes you so sure there'll be a next time? If those *macarons* turn out perfectly I won't need your help again.'

'You still need to master the filling—not to mention the assembling of the tower.'

Heck.

'And if I hear you make one more disparaging remark about your appearance I promise you, Jo, you *will* be sorry.'

She believed him. He looked utterly and completely forbidding.

* * *

Mac wasn't sure if anything had ever satisfied him as much as the gobsmacked expression plastered across Jo's face.

He leaned in closer to her again. 'You are divine, desirable, and all I can think about is kissing you. And more. *So* much more.'

'Stop.' Her voice came out as a hoarse whisper.

'You know how to make me stop, my beautiful, *beautiful* Jo.'

Her eyes widened. He could see the struggle she had not to open her mouth and contradict him. His heart twisted at the uncertainty that flashed in her eyes, at the vulnerability she tried to hide. She was one of the most beautiful women he'd ever met and it hurt something inside him that she doubted her loveliness like this.

'You have a face that poets have only ever dreamed of,' he continued. 'And, speaking of dreams...I dream constantly of unbuttoning your shirt and freeing your pretty breasts from your bra, feasting my gaze on them until I can't resist, until I lose control and have to touch them, taste them, caress them. I want to give you the same physical pleasure I get from just looking at you. Oh, and, Jo...I dream of you losing control and—'

Her lips slammed to his and Mac was determined to kiss her until she finally believed she was beautiful.

Except her lips touched his and every thought, his very ability to think, dissolved as if rational thought had never existed. All that was left was sensation. Kissing Jo was like standing on a storm-tossed headland, with the wind whipping past and thunder clapping overhead and lightning creating jagged patterns across the sky. It was crazy and elemental and not to be withstood.

He didn't try to withstand it. He'd never felt more alive in all his life.

He curved his hands around her face to deepen the kiss.

'No hands,' she murmured against his lips, before her tongue tangled with his and her hands went to the back of his neck to pull him closer.

Where he was hard she was soft. Where he was famished she spread a banquet at his feet. Where he thirsted, she bathed him in water until he felt quenched. He never wanted to stop. Kissing Jo didn't just make him feel alive. It made him feel free.

He groaned when she eventually reefed herself out of his arms. She stood there staring at him, her chest rising and falling and her fingers pressed to swollen lips. He reached out a hand to her, but she backed up and shook her head.

'Did I hurt you?' he managed to croak out.

She pulled her hand away. 'Of course not. I… It's just—' She tried to glare, but it didn't quite come off. 'I thought you promised me gentlemanly behaviour?'

So had he. 'I lost my head.' He glared too. 'This whole thing we decided…that kissing is a bad idea…that's a load of hogwash. Kissing you is the best idea I've ever had. I *like* kissing you, Jo. I like it a lot. I think there should be more of it.'

'No.'

'Why not?'

The glare she sent him should have withered him. 'Too complicated, remember?' she snapped.

She swung away to grab a couple of sodas from the fridge. She set the one he guessed was meant for him on the far side of the table from her. She opened hers and took a long swig. He couldn't drag his gaze from the long line of her throat. The longer he watched the thirstier he became.

'Mac, please stop looking at me like that!'

'I can't help it.'

And he didn't want to help it. Right or wrong, he

wanted to get naked with Jo as soon as humanly possible.

'I want you and I love looking at you.'

She scrubbed a hand down her face. 'You're deliberately trying to make this as difficult as possible.'

'My body is on fire. If you want to call a halt to things, then fine. That's your prerogative. But I want your body burning as badly as mine.'

And he could tell from the tight way she held herself that it was. There was a remarkably simple solution to that. She just had to say the word. He continued to gaze at her with naked hunger, hoping she'd lose control and kiss him again.

If he asked, would she stay? Here at the beach house? With him? He'd just made *macarons* and the world hadn't caved in. Maybe—

'Fine,' she snapped. 'I'll simply remove myself from your presence.'

'You can't. You have *macarons* in the oven.'

'Then *you* go somewhere else. Take Bandit for a walk or do some work.'

He shook his head, his eyes never leaving hers. 'My house. I can go where I want.'

Her chin shot up and those smoky eyes blazed at him. His mouth watered.

'You're determined to remain here with me in the kitchen?'

In answer he merely reached out and took possession of his can of soda.

She slammed herself into a chair. 'Fine, then I'll raise something that's been playing in my mind about Ethan.'

Was she trying to tick him off? Fine. She might find it harder than she thought. 'And what might that be?'

'Just for a moment reverse your and Ethan's situations. Pretend he's the boss and you're the apprentice.'

He dragged a hand down his face. If only that were the truth. If only—

'Imagine you're the apprentice who screwed up—as apprentices do. Wouldn't you want to see your boss? For starters, wouldn't you want to know he was okay? And, secondly, wouldn't you want to know he thought you important enough to visit?'

Bile burned his stomach. Jo turned him on like no other woman ever had, but she was going to give him an ulcer too.

'Or would I just be glad to never have to clap eyes again on the man who ruined my life?'

She folded her arms. 'Would you believe your

life was ruined? And if you did would you hold anyone else responsible?'

He had no idea, but according to Diana Devlin he had indeed ruined her son's life.

'Mac.' Jo rested her forearms on the table, her eyes dark and troubled. 'It occurred to me the other day that Ethan might, in fact, be plagued with the same guilt that torments you.'

Every muscle he had froze.

'*He's* the one who accidentally let a platter of seafood slide into that vat of oil. *He's* the direct cause for the start of the fire. You know it was an accident, and I know it was an accident, but does Ethan? Or does he hold *himself* responsible for the whole sorry mess?'

The thought horrified him. 'He can't!'

'Says who?' She stabbed a finger at him. 'How would *you* feel if the positions were reversed?'

His mouth went dry. How *would* he feel if he'd been the one who'd dropped the iced seafood into the hot oil? *Guilty as sin.* His fingers tightened around his can of soda, crushing it. Bubbles fizzed up and over his hand to drip to the floor.

He barely knew Ethan. They'd probably spoken a grand total of twenty words to each other.

Like most of the new apprentices he'd been in awe of Mac.

Mac cursed himself anew for not taking more time to put Ethan at ease for his first couple of appearances on the show.

Jo came to stand in front of him. She smelled of sugar and *macaron* and soda. 'You want me to believe I'm beautiful.'

'Because you're gorgeous,' he croaked out.

'And in the same way I want you to realise you're not responsible for the accident.'

His heart thudded. His temples pounded. And an ache started up behind his eyes. 'Ethan's not responsible either.'

'No, he's not. It was just an awful accident. I just hope he's not lying in that godforsaken hospital bed of his beating himself up about it.'

So did he.

'Mac, you just helped me make *macarons*.' She shook her head. 'If we're being honest, *you* made them. And the world didn't come tumbling down around your ears, did it?'

It took all his strength to swallow rather than howl. 'What are you trying to say?'

'I'm saying ring him.'

But Mrs Devlin said…

This mattered too much for him to get it wrong. He *had* to find out if Ethan blamed himself. If he did then Mac had to do everything he could to make the younger man see sense. To put his mind to rest.

'Mac?'

'I don't want to do anything to make matters worse.'

She handed him a tea towel to wipe his hands. Taking his can from him, she set it on the table before wiping the spill at his feet. When the oven timer buzzed it made them both jump.

He stood frozen as she pulled the tray from the oven and set it on the table.

'Your rows are perfect.' She pointed. 'Look.'

He stared at them and something inside him swelled at their perfection, at the knowledge that he'd made them.

'Mine are less so.'

'Practice. All you need, Jo, is practice.' Practice at making perfect rounds. Practice at believing she was beautiful.

I want you to realise you're not responsible for the accident.

Could she be right? He was too afraid to believe it—too afraid that Ethan would take one look at him and turn away in disgust. But what if he didn't?

His heart pounded so hard it hurt.

Jo gestured to the *macarons* and then around the kitchen. 'You love all this.'

It was pointless denying it. She'd put that whisk in his hand and for a moment he'd felt as if he could fly. He'd tried to ignore it by focussing on her story about her family, but no matter how much he'd lied to himself it hadn't worked. In much the same way it appeared that trying to turn his back on his passion hadn't worked. He could blame his talent and his ambition all he liked, but it didn't stop him from loving cooking as much as he ever had.

'I expect Ethan must love all this too.'

Something inside him stilled.

She blew out a breath and fell into a chair. 'I understand you wanting to help him. You've both suffered a dreadful accident that's changed your lives. But…'

Mac sat too, his mind a whirlwind. 'This is a hell of a way to stop me from kissing you again.'

She bit her lip. 'I shouldn't have started this. It's none of my business.'

He didn't know if he was angry with her, or grateful, or something else entirely. 'Don't stop now.'

She stared at him, her eyes dark. 'We've got in each other's faces so much this last fortnight, with me demanding you take better care of yourself and you taking issue with my body image, and me wanting to change your view of the accident and you trying to help me find a new direction career-wise. And then there's Bandit, which has added a whole new dimension. I didn't know any of this was going to happen, Mac, and it's been intense. I've never experienced this kind of intensity with anyone in such a short time before.'

He dragged a hand down his face.

She straightened, her voice suddenly tart. 'And you needn't interpret that as me being in love with you, or something stupid like that, because that's not what I'm talking about. This is... It's not friendship, but there are elements of that. It's not lust, though that's part of it.'

She shook her head. 'Maybe it's the proximity and the isolation and the fact we've both recently been through something big that's created a kind of melting pot here.' Her chin lifted. 'Do you know what I'm talking about or am I just—?'

'No.'

She glanced down at her hands.

'I mean yes,' he growled, wanting to wipe that look from her face. 'I was saying no to your alternative. I'm saying yes, I understand what you're trying to say. I can't explain it but there's a connection.'

And he didn't want there to be one. Even though he liked her.

She grasped at the air, as if searching for the right words. Her gaze returned to his—troubled, puzzled, dazed. 'When I think about some of the things I've said to you I'm appalled at myself. I don't feel like this—the here and now we're in—is the real world.'

He eased back in his seat. His heart thudded in his ears. 'There's something else you want to say that you wouldn't normally say in *the real world*, as you put it—isn't there?'

She slumped back before straightening again. 'What the heck? In for a penny… Helping Ethan realise there's a future—that he has a future to look forward to—wouldn't that be a fine way to help him?'

Yes. Yes, it would.

'You both share a passion for cooking, right?

Well, maybe Ethan would like to help you work on the cookbook.'

'He's still in hospital. He's still recovering.'

She ignored that. 'Maybe down the track the two of you could start up your own cooking show on TV—do it the way it should've been done in the first place.'

His heart tried to pound out of his chest. He leapt from his chair. 'We'd be considered freaks.'

'Is that how you see Ethan?'

Of course it wasn't. But the general public wouldn't be so kind.

'Is that how you see yourself?'

A fist tightened about his ribcage

'You tell me I'm beautiful and expect me to believe you, but you refuse to see yourself fairly.'

He was scarred. End of story.

But he didn't repel her. He met her gaze and swallowed. Maybe other people would see past his and Ethan's scars too.

'Call him, Mac. See how he's doing. Give him something to live for.'

She folded her arms when he didn't say anything. He *couldn't* say anything. A lump the size of a frozen pizza throbbed in his throat.

'Promise me you'll at least think about it?'

He gave a curt nod, feeling bruised all over.

'And tomorrow I think we should try something different. Tomorrow *you'll* come down here and cook one of your complicated recipes, barking your instructions as you go, and I'll jot them down.'

Did he dare?

'Mac, it's time to decide what's more important—your self-imposed punishment or getting this cookbook written.'

With that she left.

Mac fell back into his seat. He let out a long, slow breath from cramped lungs. Man, that really had been one hell of a way to stop him kissing her.

CHAPTER NINE

THE NEXT DAY Jo swept, vacuumed and beat rugs. She did three loads of laundry, washed dishes and wiped down shelves. She cleaned windows—inside and out. This close to the coast, the easterly sea breezes laced the windows with salt. They needed cleaning. *A lot.*

She tried to fill her mind with salt, dust and cleaning, but over and over it returned to Mac and yesterday's kiss, to the words Mac had spoken, to the hunger in his eyes. And every single time her heart fluttered up into her throat, her thighs softened and her eyes burned. Did he really think her beautiful?

She collapsed on the top step of the veranda and stared at the glorious scene in front of her, hugging a bottle of window cleaner and a cleaning cloth to her chest. She could look at it any way she wanted, but Mac wasn't feigning his desire for her. She might not be able to explain the attraction between them, but that didn't make it any less real. He found her attractive. *Beautiful.*

He wanted her.

You are divine, desirable and all I can think about is kissing you.

When he'd said that he'd made her believe it. Hearing his voice in her head now made her believe it. When she saw herself reflected in his eyes she liked what she saw. He had no reason to lie. So why couldn't she keep on believing it?

Her heart did a strange little skip.

Bandit came to sit beside her and even tolerated it when Jo fondled her ears. 'Has he shut you out too, girl?'

Jo hadn't clapped eyes on Mac once so far today and…she glanced at her watch…it was nearly three o'clock. He'd been down for coffee while she'd been pegging clothes on the line—and he'd taken the entire pot back upstairs with him. He'd obviously made himself sandwiches and taken them back up to his room too, while she'd vacuumed the front rooms. She knew he was up there. She'd heard his heavy footfalls as he'd paced back and forth, back and forth.

She scowled. It was time for him to come out of this self-imposed exile and live again.

'If he doesn't come down to cook one of those absurd recipes of his, Bandit, then he's getting fish fingers for dinner.'

'Now, *that* would be a fate worse than death.'

Bandit raced across to the door.

Jo took her time turning around.

It still didn't ready her for the shocking bolt of heat that stabbed through her. She found herself repeating over and over: *One-night stands are bad. One-night stands are bad.*

She didn't mean to be judgmental. One-night stands were all well and good between consenting adults. But instinct warned her that a fling with Mac would be a *very* bad idea. He made her feel too much. Which was a real shame, because she'd be prepared to pay a lot for the physical release he could give her, but in this instance she suspected the price would be too high.

'How are you on this fine day, Jo?'

Was it a fine day? She went to rise, but he motioned for her to remain where she was before taking a seat beside her.

'I was hoping you were about to put me to work,' she said. 'That would make it a fine day.' His eyes suddenly gleamed and she choked. She wanted to add, *In the kitchen—writing down your recipes...* but decided it would be wiser to remain silent.

'Soon,' he said, growing sober. 'I think the suggestion you made yesterday has a lot of merit. So I'll cook and you can make notes.'

Yes! And tomorrow she'd hassle him to show her how to assemble the *macaron* tower. 'Smart move. It'll save you from the fish fingers.'

'First I want to clear the air about yesterday's kiss.'

Was that even possible?

'Or at least try to explain myself.'

The shrivelling started—the dying inside. She stared directly out in front of her. Here it came—the let-her-down-gently speech. For a short time she'd believed... She shook her head and swallowed.

'I don't want you to think I want a fling with you, Jo.'

Ditto. But she remained silent. She didn't have the heart to take part in the conversation. If she had the energy she'd cut him off and ask if they couldn't just get on with the cooking.

'I like you, Jo. I like you a lot. And, yes, I want to make love with you. But you deserve more than that.'

Yeah, right. Blah, blah, blah.

'*I* want more than that.'

She frowned. That wasn't part of the usual routine. Where was he going with this?

He bumped her shoulder gently with his. 'I want more than that with *you*, Jo.'

She blinked. She blinked at the beach, at a flock of seagulls, at the field of native grass.

'Are you ever going to look at me?'

She turned to meet his gaze—his deadly earnest and vulnerable gaze. She had to swallow before she could speak. 'You're saying… Are you saying you want to pursue a relationship with me?'

'Yes.'

Something inside her started to sing.

'But…' he added.

The singing stopped. A weight dropped down on her. She swung back to face the front.

'For heaven's sake, Jo, I'm not trying to blow you off. I'm trying to tell you how I mean to go forward from here. I…I understand that I might not figure in your plans for the future, and that just because a relationship with you is what I want, it doesn't mean you're going to fall in line with me.'

She had to look at him. She couldn't help it.

He was glaring down at his clenched fists, the

pulse at the side of his jaw was throbbing, and his mouth was pressed into a thin line. This man… Her heart gave a giant kick. This man was tied up in knots. Over *her*!

She swallowed. 'You know I want you, Mac.'

Blue eyes lasered into hers.

'And I suspect you know that I like you too?'

He gave a cautious nod.

'So keep talking—because, believe me, I'm all ears.'

He straightened, and then he smiled, and it pierced through to the centre of her.

He reached out and took her hand, wrapped it between both his own. 'There are some things I need to clear up before I'm free to follow my heart.'

'Ethan?'

'I need to make sure he's okay. I need to help him in any way I can.'

He wouldn't be the man he was if he didn't want that. She wouldn't like him half so much otherwise. *Like?* Oh, yes, she liked him a lot. A whole lot. And in this particular moment that thought didn't scare her.

'I have to go see him.'

Wow. She straightened.

'I mean to leave tomorrow. I'm not sure how

long I'll be gone.' His hand tightened about hers. 'I'm not sure...'

'You're not sure...?' she pressed when he hesitated.

'If you're prepared to wait.' He stared at their interlaced hands. 'I don't know if you're prepared to wait until I return from seeing him. I'm not sure you're prepared to wait and see what my life and career may or may not develop into.' He lifted his gaze to hers, his eyes dark. 'Before the accident I could've offered you the world. But now, Jo, I don't have anything solid to offer you.'

She didn't need anything solid. 'I'll wait until you return from seeing Ethan.' A grin broke through her. 'I mean *someone* needs to keep an eye on Bandit. After that we can take it step by step.'

Once Mac and Ethan had settled on a plan of action, then she and Mac could look to the future. *Their* future.

He lifted her hand and pressed a kiss into her palm, his lips firm and warm. 'Thank you.'

Something inside her soared free then. She had a feeling the only thing that kept her anchored to the ground was Mac's touch.

They should go inside and start cooking. Knowing Mac, he'd have chosen something that would take ages to prepare, but she didn't have the heart—or the strength—to break the spell that wove around them. She imagined that in years to come she'd remember sitting here with him like this, holding hands in the mild winter sunlight, with the sound of the surf in her ears and the promise of their future in front of them.

'What are you hoping will happen with Ethan?' she finally asked.

'That he'll work on a couple of projects with me when he's ready to.'

'That sounds nice.'

'I'll move back to the city so we can do that. And so I can see you.'

'That sounds even nicer.' She tightened her hand in his. 'So far it sounds as if we're on the same page.'

He pressed another kiss into her palm. She wished he'd kiss her properly, but she knew why he didn't. If they kissed they'd lose control.

'I bless the day you came here, Jo. You've made me see possibilities I hadn't considered.'

She leaned against him, relishing his warmth and strength. 'You were grieving. You were mourning the life you'd had that was suddenly snatched away, and you were mourning for Ethan and *his* life too. Grief is a process, and you're finding a way through it.'

'Thanks to you.'

His eyes held so much promise it was all she could do not to throw herself into his arms and seek an answer to the desire coursing through her. She'd wait. Because it was what Mac wanted and perhaps what he needed. But when he finally felt free there'd be nothing to hold either of them back. Her skin tightened at the thought.

'You…uh…?' She swallowed and tried to think of something—anything—other than getting naked with Mac. 'You mean to drive your car?'

'I guess.'

'It's a pretty visible car, Mac. The Sydney paparazzi know it, don't they?'

He grimaced. 'I'll hire something.'

And someone somewhere would leak that too. Mac deserved to embark on his mission free from the worries of the press.

'You can borrow The Beast if you want. Nobody'll look twice at you in that.'

'You'd trust me with your car?'

'As you'll be leaving your gorgeous sports car here, in my care, trusting you with The Beast only seems fair.' She was going to trust him with her heart. In comparison, her car was nothing.

He laughed. 'Deal.'

And then he leant forward and touched his lips to hers. He tasted of coffee and determination, and his kiss tasted like every promise she'd been too afraid to wish for.

It ended far too soon, but she knew why. The spark between them was already too hot, too twitchy. They had to negotiate it carefully or—

Stop thinking about getting naked with Mac!

'You're beautiful, Jo.'

She didn't contradict him. She didn't want to. 'You make me feel beautiful.'

His smile was her reward. 'You don't know the half of how beautiful I'm going to make you feel.'

She groaned. A sound of need and frustration she had no hope of holding back.

He nodded. 'I'm hoping I won't be gone too long.'

So was she.

He rose, pulling her to her feet. 'Come on—it's time to cook.'

'What are we cooking?'

'*Macarons.* I have a good recipe for them—better than the one you were using yesterday—and you need to keep practising.'

She all but floated into the kitchen with him.

* * *

Mac left at the crack of dawn the next day.

Leaving Jo behind when all he wanted to do was make love to her, prove to her over and over again how beautiful she was, was one of the hardest things he'd ever done.

He gritted his teeth, resisting the increasingly urgent craving. He had nothing to offer her. Nothing solid. No kind of future. But a future might be possible, mightn't it? A future could be wrestled from the wreckage the accident had wrought.

He held to the thought tightly, because he ached for that future. With Jo.

He tapped his fingers against the steering wheel and wondered what she'd be doing. She'd planned to make more *macarons*. The thought made him smile, because she didn't even like them. She'd taken a bite from one yesterday and with an 'Ugh!' had tossed it in the bin. She'd planned to take yesterday's batch to the farm where she bought the eggs.

'Maybe someone will find a use for them.'

That was what she'd said. He laughed. The very thought of her warmed him to the soles of his feet in a way he could never have imagined a month ago. Beautiful, breath-of-fresh-air Jo, who'd breezed into his life and turned it upside down like some kind of super-heroine from a comic book.

Imagining Jo in a skimpy superhero outfit kept him pleasantly engaged for half an hour. Especially when he imagined peeling it from her gorgeous body.

He spent another hour wondering what kind of dessert would make her mouth truly water. If she didn't like *macarons* then anything too meringuey was off the list. He selected dessert after dessert, only to dismiss them. Eventually he grinned. Maybe pineapple upside-down cake? *Yes.* Something warm and rich and full of flavour. That would suit her perfectly.

As soon as he returned to the beach house he'd make her one. He'd watch every nuance of her expression as she ate it. He could spend a lifetime making food to indulge all her senses. She'd appreciate his efforts too. He had no doubt about that. And he'd relish her relish.

Before he knew it the five-hour drive to Sydney was almost complete. He could hardly wait to return to Jo, but first things first.

He drove over the Sydney Harbour Bridge, but he didn't head for his swanky inner-city apartment. He turned the car in the opposite direction—towards Ethan's private clinic.

Jo pulled her phone from her pocket to glance at it for the umpteenth time, but there were no new messages, no new texts.

In the last two days she'd sent Mac five texts. She grimaced at Bandit, who lay under the kitchen table with her nose between her front paws, evidently missing Mac too.

'Do you think five texts is too many, Bandit? Too needy?'

Jo collapsed into a chair. She flipped out one finger. 'Are you there yet?' She held out a second finger. 'Thinking of you.' She stared at a third finger. 'Sunny and fine here.' She grimaced at the fourth. 'Missing you. Ugh! Now, *that*, Bandit, was too much.'

She dropped her hand to her lap. Her last message had been a simple goodnight before she'd gone to sleep last night.

She straightened. She wouldn't be needy. Mac had a plan he needed to bring off, and in the meantime he'd asked her to wait. She'd wait—because his eyes had promised that once he'd done what he needed to do he'd devote all the time she wanted— needed—to her...to them.

She hugged herself. She still found it hard to believe that Mac wanted her.

And she wanted him.

Oh, what was the point in denying it? Somewhere along the line she'd fallen in love with him. She couldn't pinpoint the exact moment. Their first kiss? Their second? When they'd argued about fish fingers? When he'd helped her polish off that pizza? The scorn in his eyes for her cruel excuse of an ex-boyfriend?

Thanks to Mac, she saw that for what it was now—the attempt of a sad bunch of losers with no self-esteem to build themselves up at the expense of others.

Pitiful.

It was pitiful that she'd let it affect her for so long too, but it had fed into all the insecurities created by her grandmother and her great-aunt. She let out a long breath. It had been easier to believe that she was unattractive than to risk being vulnerable again. Well, no more. She set her shoulders. She'd never fall into that pattern again. Living with that kind of fear emotionally crippled a person, and life was too short.

'Way too short, Bandit.'

She stood and swiped a bottle of water from the fridge, then headed for the front veranda. She turned in the doorway. 'C'mon, Bandit—the fresh air will do you good.'

Bandit huffed out from beneath the table, head hanging low as she scuffed after Jo. When they reached the veranda Jo bent down to caress Bandit's face.

'Aw, honey, he'll be home soon.'

She sat and glanced out at the view. In the meantime she meant to savour her newfound sense of self. She was done with feeling like a freak. She was done with feeling as if she was too tall, too large, too broad—too anything! By whose standards was she any of those things? Even the tiny, gorgeous women who adorned the covers of magazines were airbrushed to within an inch of their lives—their eyes widened, their necks lengthened, their waists trimmed and their thighs shrunk.

What was *that* about? If the so-called beautiful people weren't beautiful enough, then what hope did real people like her have? None. Because the standard was no longer human—it was in the mind of some designer and that was where the real freakishness lay. She was done with trying to live up to such impossible standards.

From now on she meant to wear whatever she wanted to wear—dresses, heels, chunky jewellery—regardless of whether it drew attention or not. She was healthy, she was strong, and she was a good person. She was kind to animals and to moody men. She was independent and able to make her own way in the world.

Mac desired her, wanted her, but she could see now that too was secondary. It didn't matter what anyone else thought. It only mattered what she thought of herself.

She threw her arms out wide and lifted her face to the sun. 'I am beautiful!' She yelled the words at the top of her lungs and then with a laugh cracked open her water. 'If anyone hears me, Bandit, they'll think I'm a certified nutcase.'

Bandit, who'd collapsed by the door, flicked an ear in Jo's direction, but nothing more.

Jo pointed a finger at her. 'Now, you have to stop being a pathetic female, Bandit. Seriously—neediness is a bad look.'

Nothing. No response at all.

'It's never wise to pin all your hopes on a man.' She wrinkled her nose and grimaced. Well, on that count both she and Bandit had failed. Spectacularly. 'Except we can trust Mac, Bandit.' She swallowed and nodded. 'He's a man among men.'

Bandit's head lifted. Jo stared at the dog and pushed her shoulders back with a proud little shuffle. Well, well… Perhaps Bandit listened to her after all. Maybe she wasn't as indifferent to Jo as she pretended to be.

'I mean Mac won't let either one of us down, and—'

She broke off when Bandit leapt to her feet with a joyful bark and scampered down the steps at full speed. What on earth…?

'Bandit, you have a tummy full of puppies!' she hollered. 'You need to be careful!'

And then she heard it too. A car coming up the drive.

Her heart started to thud. Mac was home? She bounced upright, spilling water. She wanted to race towards the sound in the same way Bandit had.

Pride, she lectured herself, leaning against a veranda post as if she hadn't a care in the world. She did her best not to bounce. She had no hope whatsoever of keeping the smile from her face, though. *Mac was home!* She couldn't wait to hear a about the plans he and Ethan had made. She wanted Mac to be filled with hopes and dreams and plans for the future. She meant to figure large there.

Mac manoeuvred the car along the rutted driveway. He didn't stop to let Bandit into the cab—which, given Bandit's over-the-top exuberance, was probably wise. Jo remained leaning against her post even when he pulled the car to a halt at the front of the house.

She wanted him to see her standing there, tall and proud in the sunlight, elevated by the veranda, and she wanted to make him hungrier than he'd ever been in his life.

When he pushed out of the car, though, that thought fled. She raced down the steps towards him, appalled at his pallor and at the darkness that seemed to drag his eyes deep into their sockets. She took his arm. She'd have hugged him, but he shook her off.

'Not now, Jo.'

She tried not to take it personally. 'You look ill. Do you need a doctor?'

He shook his head.

'Then how about you put your feet up and I'll get you a sandwich and a beer?'

'I'm going to take a shower.'

He hadn't even taken the time to pet Bandit, but he did let the dog follow at his heels.

Lucky Bandit.

Mac and the dog disappeared inside the house. Jo lowered herself back to the step. Things had evidently not gone well in Sydney.

She closed her eyes. *Patience.* She'd let him shower and rest without pestering him, and later she'd put some good food in his belly. By then he might be ready to talk. Between them they'd find a solution to this setback.

She pushed to her feet. Spaghetti and meatballs. Comfort food. That was what they needed.

Mac closed his eyes as the stinging spray from the shower rained down on him, but he couldn't get the image of Ethan out of his mind. That image was burned there to torment him for all eternity.

Six months on and the nineteen-year-old still had to wear a bodysuit, was still in pain. Mac closed his eyes and braced his arms against the tiles.

Six months might have passed, but Ethan had taken one look at Mac and growled, 'Go away,' before turning his back.

Six years—sixty years—wouldn't be enough to erase the harm Mac had done.

And then Diana Devlin had walked in and it had all gone to hell in a handbasket from there.

He scrubbed shampoo through his hair, digging his fingers into his scalp, wishing he could trade places with Ethan, if only for a day, to give him some respite.

Ethan's doctor had taken time to talk to Mac. Mac had well and truly wanted out of there by that time—going to visit Ethan had been a grave mistake—but the doctor had at least been able to assure him that the upset wouldn't impede Ethan's recovery.

That was something, at least.

In fact the doctor had said Ethan's recovery was going better than any of them had hoped. He'd even implied that Ethan could have gone home weeks ago.

Ethan hadn't wanted to. The doctor hadn't said as much, but Mac had read between the lines. They were keeping him in for 'psychological assessment'—those had been the actual words. Not unusual in these circumstances, as it happened.

Mac twisted the taps off and seized a towel, scrubbing it over his face and hair. They thought Ethan was in danger of committing suicide. No wonder Diana hated him.

The accident hadn't just damaged Ethan phys-ically. It had damaged him mentally. That was Mac's fault.

An ache stretched his throat. He'd never be free from that. *Never.*

He threw down the towel and dressed in the nearest things to hand—worn jeans and a faded sweater. The days of bespoke suits and designer clothes were behind him. He stood at the window and stared out. Eventually he roused himself and spun back to face the room.

He hung up his towel, put his dirty laundry in the washing basket, unpacked.

You can't put off going downstairs forever.

Weight slammed to his shoulders then, threat-ening to crush him. Earlier, when he'd pulled the car to a halt at the front of the house and had seen Jo standing in the sunshine, proud and magnifi-cent, his chest had cracked open and split down the middle like a hewn log.

He paced from one side of the room to the other, hands clenched and muscles corded. For as long as he owed such a debt to Ethan he didn't have the right to pursue his own happiness. He pushed both hands back through his hair, fighting for breath.

What he had to focus on was making enough money to ensure Ethan was looked after.

The dreams he'd started to dream—they were dust. It was what he deserved.

But Jo? She deserved better.

He pressed his palms to hot eyes and eased himself down to the edge of the bed.

Mac forced himself downstairs for dinner. Food was the last thing on his mind, but he didn't doubt for one moment that if he didn't appear Jo would storm upstairs to demand an explanation.

The concern in her eyes when he strode into the kitchen cut him to the quick. 'I'm fine,' he bit out before she could ask.

He took the jug of iced water and two glasses she had sitting on the kitchen bench through to the dining room. She followed a few moments later with a fragrant platter of spaghetti and meatballs.

She dished them out generous servings, but she didn't start to eat. She gulped down water, the glass wobbling precariously in her hold.

'I take it your trip didn't go precisely as you'd hoped?'

It hurt him to look at her, but he forced himself

to do it all the same. He deserved to throb and burn. 'He's a mess, Jo.'

'He's been through a lot.'

'Seeing me didn't help. Seeing me just made things worse.'

'How…?' Her voice was nothing more than a whisper.

He had to pull in a breath before he could continue. 'He hates the sight of me.'

She didn't say anything. She sliced into a meatball, slathered it in sauce and ate it. Her lips closed about the morsel and need rose up in him so hard that wind rushed in his ears, deafening him. Seizing his knife and fork he attacked a meatball, reducing it to a pile of mush. He started in on a second one and then on the spaghetti.

'I can put that in the blender for you if it's how you'd prefer to eat it.'

He set his cutlery down, afraid he wouldn't be able to push food past the lump in his throat. His stomach churned too hard for food anyway.

Jo continued to eat, as if unaware of his mental turmoil. He wasn't stupid enough to believe that, though. She was eating to stave off heartbreak. A fist reached out and squeezed his chest, all but cutting off his air supply.

'So,' she said eventually, with a toss of her head, not meeting his gaze. 'What's the plan from here?'

His very heartbeat seemed to slow. It was all he could do not to drop his head to the table.

From a long way away he heard himself say, 'I revert back to Plan A.'

Her gaze flew to his and he watched with a sickening thud as realisation dawned in those sage eyes. Her eyebrows drew in and she gripped a fistful of her shirt right above her heart.

He swallowed and forced himself to continue. 'I focus on making enough money to take care of every single one of Ethan's needs for as long as he needs me to.'

'I...' With a physical effort she swallowed, but she didn't loosen the grip on her shirt. 'Where does that leave us?'

Bile burned like acid in his throat, coating his tongue. 'There can't be an "us", Jo. At least not for the foreseeable future.'

She stared at him for long, pain-filled seconds, as if she hadn't heard him properly, and then she flinched as if he'd struck her. The colour leached from her face; the creases about her eyes deepened. Heaviness settled over him. His chin edged down towards his chest. His heart was thudding dully there. How could he have done this to her? Why hadn't he taken more care?

I'm sorry! The words screamed through him, but he couldn't force them out.

She swung back, eyes blazing. 'You fall at the first hurdle and give up? Come running home with your tail between your legs?'

He wanted to open his arms and make his body a target, to tell her to hurl whatever insults she could at him. Anything to make her feel better. Only he knew it wouldn't help. Not one jot.

'Has life always been easy for you? Have you never had to fight for anything?'

She laughed, but it wasn't the kind of laugh he ever wanted to hear again.

'Russ used to brag about you—about how you were this *wunderkind* who went from triumph to triumph.' She shot to her feet. 'But the fact of the matter is all that coming so easily for you has made you a…a *loser*!'

Her words cut at him like whips. He wanted to beg her to forgive him.

'When something really matters, Mac, you keep trying until you succeed—despite the setbacks. If Ethan really mattered to you, you'd try harder.'

What she was really saying, though, was that

if *she* mattered to him he'd fight harder for her. It was what she deserved.

As for Ethan... He shook his head. He couldn't force his presence on the young man again. He'd done enough damage as it was.

'But you're not going to do that, are you?'

How could he make her understand the extent of Ethan's misery? What was the point anyway? She'd simply tell him to do something to ease that misery. That was beyond Mac's powers. What he *could* do was make money to hire people who'd bring about a positive difference in Ethan's life.

'You're just going to give in.'

There wasn't an ounce of inflection in her voice and that was worse than her anger. Ten times worse.

She dotted her mouth with her napkin, tossed it down beside her plate, and left.

It felt as if his heart had stopped beating.

CHAPTER TEN

MAC BARELY SLEPT, but he forced himself out of bed as the first rays of sun filtered over the horizon. He made himself dress and go straight into the master bedroom. He opened the curtains to let in the light. Shutting himself up in the dark, not caring about what he ate and not getting any exercise had been stupid things to do.

He had to stay healthy.

With that thought he cracked open the glass sliding door. Air filtered in—cold but fresh.

Only then did he turn to his computer and switch it on. A hard brick settled in his stomach, but he ignored it to examine the lists of recipes he'd selected for the cookbook. At least a dozen of them were either not started or unfinished.

That meant a dozen recipes he'd have to make while barking instructions for Jo to jot down. He pulled in a breath. That was twelve days' work, if he made a recipe a day and wrote it up in the evening. Less if he did two recipes a day. On top of that there was the glossary of terms and techniques to write up, and serving suggestions to add to each recipe.

He created a table and a timeline. He printed off a shopping list for Jo. He would get to work on the first recipe this afternoon. After that he'd talk Jo through the icing she'd need to make for her *macaron* tower. She could tackle that under his supervision tomorrow morning.

He rose, collecting the shopping list from the printer on his way to the door.

'C'mon, Bandit.'

A morning and afternoon walk down to the beach each day, perhaps along it for a bit, would keep both man and dog healthy. He set the shopping list on the kitchen table before letting himself out of the house. Quietly. It was still early.

The sun rose in spectacular munificence over the Pacific Ocean, creating a path of orange and gold. At the edges of the path the water darkened to mercury and lavender. The air stood still, and with the tide on the turn the waves broke on pristine sand in a hushed rhythmic lilt.

Mac halted on a sand dune to stare at it all. It should fill his soul with glory. It should fill him with the majesty of nature. It should…

He'd give it all up for a single night in Jo's arms.

He dragged a hand down his face and tried to banish the thought. A single night wouldn't be enough for her. It wouldn't be enough for him either, but it would at least be something he could hold onto in the bleak, monotonous months to come.

He rested his hands on his knees and pulled in a breath. Except he couldn't do that to her. He laughed, although the sound held little mirth. More to the point, she wouldn't let him do it to her.

Good.

The weight across his shoulders bowed him until he knelt in the sand with Bandit's warm body pressed against him.

I can do this. I can do this. I can do this.

He lifted his head. He *had* to do this.

Forcing his shoulders back, he lumbered to his feet and stumbled along the beach for ten minutes before turning and making his way back to the house.

The scent of frying bacon hit him the moment he opened the front door. He hesitated before heading for the kitchen. Leaning a shoulder against the doorframe, he drank her in—the unconscious grace of her movements, the dark glossiness of her hair and the strength that radiated from her.

'That smells good,' he managed.

She didn't turn from the stove. 'Bacon always smells good.'

He could tell nothing of her mood or state of mind from either her posture or her tone of voice.

He rubbed his nape. 'I didn't think you were much of a breakfast person.' Mind you, she'd barely eaten any dinner last night.

'I'm not usually, but I make an exception when I'm setting off on a car journey.'

She moved to butter the toast that had popped up in the toaster and that was when Mac saw the suitcases sitting by the doorway leading out to the laundry and the back door.

A chill crept across the flesh of his arms and his face, down his back. 'You're leaving?'

'I am.'

His heart pounded. 'Today?'

'That's right.'

She finally turned. The dark circles under her eyes made him wince. She nodded at his shopping list.

'So I'm afraid you'll have to get your own groceries.'

A knife pierced through the very centre of him. She couldn't leave! Just because they couldn't be together in the way they wanted it didn't mean she had to go.

She set the toast on the table and then two plates laden with bacon, eggs and beans. She'd made enough for him too. Maybe she'd had the same thought—that he hadn't eaten much at dinner last night either. It warmed some of the chill out of him, but not for long.

When she indicated he should do so, he sat. He stared at his plate. He forced himself to eat, but all the while his mind whirled. Jo couldn't leave. He needed her here. She—

She needs to eat. Wait until after she's eaten.

Two rashers of bacon, a piece of toast and a fried egg later, he pushed his plate away. 'Thank you.'

'You're welcome.'

He waited until she'd finished before speaking again. 'Why are you leaving?'

She took their plates to the sink. She wore a pair of jeans that fitted her like a glove. Had she worn them deliberately to torment him? He gulped down his orange juice but it did nothing to quench the thirst rising through him.

She pushed a mug of coffee towards him, cradling another mug in her hands and leaning against the kitchen bench.

She took a sip before finally meeting his eyes. 'I'm leaving, Mac, because I refuse to watch you sacrifice yourself on the altar of guilt and misplaced responsibility.'

He swallowed back his panic. 'I prefer to call it duty.'

'You can call it what you like. Doesn't change the fact it's messed up.'

His head rocked back.

'And I'm not going to support you in that delusion.'

Jo might not understand what drove him, but it didn't mean she had to *leave*! 'You haven't learned how to make the *macaron* tower yet.'

She shrugged. 'I did that stupid vocational test of yours again last night.'

He closed his eyes and pinched the bridge of his nose, concentrated on breathing.

'I considered each of the questions as honestly as I could and you know what? It came back with the perfect job. So thanks for the tip.'

How would he cope out here without her?

He forced his eyes open. 'What job?' he croaked, a fist tightening about his chest.

'Paramedic.'

Saving lives? Dealing with emergencies?

She'd saved Russ's life, and probably Bandit's. She'd forced Mac to turn his life around. Her practicality, her strength, her ability to respond quickly, it made her... *Perfect.* The single word rang a death knell through hopes he hadn't realised he still harboured. Impossible hopes.

Jo deserved to get on with her life.

Without him.

He just hadn't known that letting her go would tear the heart from his chest.

'The NSW Ambulance Service is recruiting soon, so I figured it's time I got on with things.'

Mac found himself on his feet, moving towards her. He cupped her face. Her skin was warm and soft and alive against his hands.

'Stay,' he croaked. 'Please. Just another week.'

In another week he'd find the strength to let her go, but please God don't ask him to relinquish her today. *Please.*

Her eyes melted to emerald for a moment before she blinked them back to a smoky sage. 'If I stay we'll become lovers,' she whispered.

'Sounds perfect to me.'

He ached to kiss her, but she planted a hand on his chest and forced him back a step.

'To you it probably does, but I'm not going to settle for second best. I will never come first with you, Mac. Ethan always will.' She swallowed, her face pale. 'I deserve to come first with the man I choose to share my life with.'

Her words forced him back another step. His heart burned. Ethan had to come first. He had to look after the other man until he was back on his feet, and there was no telling how long that would take.

If he made a lot of money—millions of dollars—he could set up a trust fund to take care of Ethan, and then he'd be free to follow his heart.

If.

He stared down at his hands. Jo had no intention of waiting around to find out if he could manage that. He couldn't say he blamed her.

She cleaned the kitchen. He'd have told her not to bother except that would only mean she'd leave sooner. He took her bags out to The Beast and stowed them in the back. He rested his head against the doorframe before striding back into the kitchen.

'What about Bandit?'

She lifted a hand to her temple and rubbed it, making him wonder if she had a roaring headache too. 'I thought you wanted to keep her?'

He shook himself. 'I mean what about the puppies?'

She seized a tea towel, shook it out and hung it on its rack. 'When they're ready to be weaned I'll come and collect them. If there are any issues let me know. I've left my mobile number, my email address and my grandmother's contact details beside the phone in the in the hall.'

She didn't meet his eyes. Not once.

His heart started to thump—hard. 'Is that where you'll be staying?'

She slung her handbag across her shoulder. 'It's my childhood home.'

He suddenly found it difficult to swallow. He stared at that handbag. She was really leaving?

'Goodbye, Mac.'

He had to swallow the bellow that rose up inside him. They couldn't end like this! There'd been so much promise and—

She reached out as if to touch him, but her hand dropped short. 'I really do wish you well. I hope...'

What did she hope?

'I hope that you succeed.'

She spun on her heel then, and shot through the laundry and out of the back door. He lumbered after her, his limbs heavy and clumsy, as if they didn't belong to him. She was so calm, so cool and untouchable. As if she didn't care. She was tearing him to pieces.

A black knot of acid burned through the centre of him. 'Is this really so easy for you?' The words left him on a bellow. 'Don't you feel the slightest sting or throb? Don't you—?'

'Easy?' She swung towards him, her face contorting. 'Easy to walk away from dreams you let me believe were possible? Dreams that—?'

Her eyes filled and her pain rose up all around him.

'Easy?' She lifted her hands as if to beat out her pain on his chest.

He wanted to wrap her in his arms and make her pain go away, soothe the desperation in her eyes and the despair that twisted her lips.

'Jo…' He swore.

'Easy?' She thumped her chest. 'When you've broken something inside me that I'm afraid I'll never be able to fix?'

His mouth dried. His stomach knotted. He

wanted to hide from the accusation in her eyes, from the anguish there—anguish *he'd* caused.

'I'm sorry, Jo. I—'

She twisted her hands in the collar of his shirt and slammed her lips to his. The world tilted. She explored every last millimetre of his lips with a hunger that had the wind rushing in his ears, firing his every nerve-ending to life. She deepened the kiss as if her very life depended on it, and everything he had reached towards her.

But she pushed him away.

'I tried to play nice, Mac, and keep it civilised, but you made it impossible! I hope that kiss torments you every night for as long as you hole up out here.'

She needn't fear. It would burn him through all eternity. As would the tears in her eyes and the pain that turned her lips white.

'That's it, Mac. That's us done.'

She slammed into her car, started up the motor and roared away.

He stared after her, her words ringing in his ears. *That's us done.*

Behind him Bandit set up a whine that became a howl.

Mac spun around. 'You're too late, you dumb

dog. You should've told her you loved her while you had the chance.'

Mac picked up a rock and hurled it with all his might at a fencepost. He kicked a tuft of grass, jarring his ankle when he connected a little too well with it. He yelled out his pain and frustration at the top of his lungs. But it didn't help.

The end. *Finito.* This was as far as he and Jo would ever go. He stood there, arms at his sides, breathing hard. Jo was gone. The earth might as well spin off its axis for all the sense that made.

He waited for the sky to darken and a curtain to descend about him. It didn't. The sun kept shining, the breeze continued to rustle a path through the native grass, and on the beach waves kept rushing up onto the sand.

His heart shrivelled to the size of a pea.

Jo was gone.

It was his fault.

And there was nothing he could do about it.

CHAPTER ELEVEN

MAC FINISHED THE cookbook in a fortnight rather than the projected month.

A morning walk, an afternoon walk and making sure he ate three square meals a day still left him with a lot of time on his hands. So he worked.

He didn't sleep much.

He sent the manuscript off to his editor and then cleaned the house from top to bottom. Having neglected it completely since Jo had left, that took him two full days.

On the third morning after finishing the cookbook, with nothing planned for the day, he stared at the omelette he'd made for breakfast and found he couldn't manage so much as a bite. With a snarl, he grabbed his coffee and stormed out to the veranda.

Twiddling his thumbs like this was driving him crazy. When would he hear back from his editor?

He collapsed to the step and ordered himself to admire the view.

'See? Beautiful!'

His scowl only deepened. The view did nothing to ease the burn in his soul or the darkness threatening to tug him under. He'd kept himself busy for a reason. He'd missed Jo every second of every day and every night, but keeping busy had helped him to deal with it, to cope with it, to push the pain to the boundaries of his mind.

He had to find something to do. He leapt up, intending to stride down to the beach for the second time in an hour. Bandit stood too. He stared at her and pursed his lips. If he went down there she'd want to come, and with her about to drop her puppies any day she should probably be taking it easy.

He glanced around wildly for something else to do and his gaze landed on a rosebush. He nodded once. The garden needed wrestling into shape. He could wrestle while Bandit dozed in the sun.

He gathered some battered implements—a hoe, a trowel and secateurs—from the garage. He barely glanced at his car, even though he still made sure to turn the engine over twice a week. It reminded him too much of Jo.

Digging up weeds and pruning rosebushes reminded him of Jo too. Everything reminded him of Jo. He wondered how she was getting along with her *macaron* tower.

One thing about being so hung up on Jo—it meant he had less time to brood about Ethan.

Jo's voice sounded in his head. *You're just going to give up...? Fight harder...*

What else could he do? He'd make sure Ethan wanted for nothing.

Except a life.

He started reciting multiplication tables.

When lunchtime rolled around he ate cold omelette and a banana. He sat outside in the sun because the kitchen reminded him too much of Jo. So did the dining room.

'I miss her *more*,' he shot at Bandit, who moped nearby. She didn't flick so much as a whisker.

Has life always been that easy for you?

Yep. Right up until the accident. 'But don't worry, Jo—it's hell now.'

Which was unfair. Jo had only ever wanted his happiness.

Fight harder.

'How?' He shouted out the word at the top of his lungs, making Bandit start.

He apologised with a pat to her head. What did Jo mean? How could he fight any harder? He was fighting as hard as he could!

He paced the length of the garden bed. He was fighting as hard as he could to make money.

That wasn't what Jo had meant, though, was it?

He bent at the waist to rest his hands on his knees. He didn't know how to fight for Ethan when the other man hated the very sight of him. How could he rouse the younger man from his apathy and depression if—?

Mac froze. The trowel fell from his fingers. Ethan hated the sight of him in the same way Mac had loathed the idea of a housekeeper. Blackmail had been the only method that had worked on him. Blackmail and playing on his guilt about Russ.

He'd loathed the very idea of Jo, but her presence here had forced him to reassess how he was living, to question the bad habits he'd formed. He certainly hadn't welcomed her with open arms, but she hadn't gone running for the hills.

As he'd done with Ethan.

No, she'd forced his inward gaze outwards. She'd reminded him that he needed food and exercise for his body, along with sunlight and fresh air. She'd forced him to recognise that he wasn't betraying the task he'd set himself if he took the time to enjoy those things. She'd made him see that he needed those things if he was to accomplish that task.

She'd stormed in here and turned his world up-side down. He hadn't enjoyed it. He'd resisted it. But it had been good for him.

It had brought him back to life.

Who did Ethan have to give him that kind of tough love?

His mother? Very slowly Mac shook his head. Diana was too caught up in her fear for her son and her anger at the world.

From the corner of his eye he saw Bandit polish off the rest of his abandoned omelette. He didn't bother scolding her. She'd put up with his growly grumpiness and no Jo for the last fortnight too. If omelette helped, then all power to her.

Mac drummed his fingers against his thighs for a moment, before pushing his shoulders back and reaching into his pocket for his mobile phone. He punched in the number for Ethan's doctor.

Jo carefully sealed the lid on the airtight container holding the most perfect dozen *macarons* she'd ever seen. She set them gently on a shelf at the very back of the pantry with the other six dozen *macarons* she'd spent the last few days baking. She had twice as many as she needed, but she wasn't taking any chances. Each and every one of them was perfect.

All the less than perfect ones had been placed in her grandmother's biscuit tin, and even her grandmother's enthusiasm for them had started to wane. After her grandmother's birthday dinner tonight Jo would be glad if she never set eyes on another *macaron* for as long as she lived.

Puffing out a breath, she moved back to the table and pulled a plastic cone towards her. She had another eight of these cones in the cupboard. This one she was going to ice. Easy-peasy. Which was precisely what it wanted to be after the number of cones she'd already practised on.

She pushed her hair back from her face. What on earth possessed people to spend hours—or in this case days—slaving over a dish that would be demolished in a matter of minutes? Where was the satisfaction in that?

If Mac ever rang her she'd ask him.

Her throat ached, her temples throbbed and her chest cramped—as always happened whenever she thought about Mac. And as she thought about him a lot you'd think she'd be used to it by now.

She gripped her hands together. It had been eight weeks since she'd left his coastal hideaway, but she still hadn't grown used to the gaping sense of loss that yawned through her. Some days it was all she could do to get from minute to minute. Some days it was all she could do not to lie in some dark corner and shut the rest of the world out.

But what good would that do anyone?

Please! Some histrionic part of herself that tore at her hair and sobbed uncontrollably pleaded with her. *Please, can't we just...?*

Jo swallowed hard and shook her head, blinking furiously. *No, they couldn't.*

She wished she'd been able to hold onto her anger for longer. That anger had helped initially, but it had slipped away almost as soon as she'd arrived home. Instead, the hope that Mac would come to his senses had grown—the hope that he'd call her and tell her he loved her and was prepared to create a life that included her.

Which made her a certifiable idiot.

'But a beautiful idiot,' she whispered, reminding herself that her time with Mac hadn't been entirely wasted.

Of course it hadn't been wasted. By the time she'd left he'd been healthier, stronger, and sexier than sin. Whether he knew it or not, she'd been good for him.

Oh, he knew it all right. It just wasn't enough.

She collected icing sugar—the good, pure stuff—butter, milk and food colouring. The fact of the matter was she *had* heard from Mac. Twice. A curt email on the evening she'd left, asking if she'd reached her destination safely. She'd answered with an equally short Yes, thank you. And a week later he'd sent her a recipe for a *macaron* tower.

She'd thanked him again. Very briefly. And that had been the sorry extent of their communication. She expected to hear from him soon, though. Bandit must have had her puppies by now, and those puppies must be getting old enough to be weaned.

Why hadn't he let her know when Bandit had had them and how many there were? Why...?

Because he'd been too caught up in whatever his latest scheme was for making money for Ethan, that was why.

She seized the plastic cone and snapped it in half. She dug her fingernails into it and gouged and shredded until some of the frustration eased out of her. Then she calmly retrieved another one and set it on the table. She pulled in a breath.

Okay, now she was ready to start.

The doorbell rang, but Jo ignored it. It would

simply be more flowers for her grandmother. Her grandmother could answer it.

Jo set about measuring icing sugar.

Grandma popped her head into the kitchen a moment later. 'Jo, dear, would you mind coming out for a moment? We have a visitor.'

'Is it Great-Aunt Edith?' Had she dropped in early for some reason?

'No, dear, and I don't believe it's an emissary sent by her to sabotage the making of your *macaron* tower either.'

Your macaron *tower*. But Jo remained silent. Her great-aunt mightn't like losing, but she'd never stoop to foul play. Her grandmother, however, had taken to imagining dastardly plots at every turn.

Wiping her hands down the front of her shirt, Jo walked out into the lounge room—and her hands froze at rib level when she saw who stood there.

Mac!

She stared, mouth agape. It took all her strength to snap it closed again, and the blood pounded in her ears and she had to plant her feet to counter the sudden giddiness that swirled through her.

She glanced at her grandmother, who smiled serenely.

She glanced at Mac, who smiled serenely.

Serene? Her heart tried to pound a path out of her chest. She wanted to scream. Whether in joy or despair, though, she wasn't sure.

'Hello, Jo.'

She swallowed and released the lip she'd been biting. 'What are you doing here, Mac?'

'Didn't I say, dear?' Grandma patted her arm. 'I've hired Mac to cater my dinner.'

She'd *what*? 'But…how?'

'I rang to tell you about the puppies, but you weren't in.'

Grandma hadn't mentioned that!

'We got talking. Your grandmother asked me if I'd be interested in catering her birthday dinner. And…' He shrugged.

It took every last muscle she had not to dissolve in the warmth of his eyes. The heat between them was as blistering as ever. She gripped her hands together. It would be a bad idea. Becoming lovers with this man would make her miserable.

You're already miserable.

She tossed her head and hardened her heart. 'And…?' she persisted.

'And I found I couldn't refuse.'

She would *not* be his consolation prize.

She opened her mouth, a set-down on her lips, but Mac had turned away to rifle in a basket.

He turned back with a handful of squirming fluffy puppy, wearing a pink and green bow around its neck. 'Happy birthday, Lucinda.'

'Oh, my word. Edith will have a fit!' Her grandmother clapped her hands in delight. 'Thank you, Malcolm, what a lovely gift.'

Jo tried to prevent her eyes from starting from her head.

'And this one here is for you, Jo. I've called her Beauty.'

He placed the puppy in her arms and she had to close her eyes as his familiar scent hit her and the warmth of his voice threatened to cast a spell about her.

She took a step away from him. Liking each other had never been their problem. It was only logical that he'd still like her as much as he ever had—want her as much as he ever had. What wasn't logical was her instant response to him, given all that had happened—or not happened—between them.

It had been two months. She shouldn't love him as much now as she had then. She wanted to weep, only it filled her with so much joy to see him.

You'll pay for it tomorrow.

Her eyes stung. She moved further away from him, from all the temptation and remembered pain, to perch on an armchair with her sweet, sleepy puppy.

'Believe it or not...'

She couldn't help but glance up.

'Bandit has been pining for you.'

Only Bandit? She shook her head. 'I don't believe you.'

On the other side of the room her grandmother cooed over her puppy. Beauty snuggled down on Jo's lap, taking the base of Jo's thumb into her mouth as if determined to keep a hold of her. Jo covered her body with her free hand to let her know she was loved.

'The moment you left she set up a whine that turned into a howl.'

Truly? She gestured for him to take a seat on the sofa opposite, but he didn't move from where he stood. He all but devoured her with his hot, hungry gaze. She rolled her shoulders and swallowed.

'She hasn't forgiven me yet for letting you leave.'

Jo would. Forgive him, that was. If he said he was sorry and asked her to return with him she would. In an instant

No! That would be a bad thing, remember? She had a life. She'd have a new job soon. She had a puppy.

But she didn't have Mac.

You can't have everything.

She lifted her chin. 'Good for her.' She was *not* going to sacrifice her life to a man intent on sacrificing his own life to guilt and regret.

'How's Ethan?' It was a nasty little dart, but they both needed to remember why they couldn't be together.

'He's doing okay. I left him and Diana out at the beach house.'

He'd what?

Her jaw dropped. The puppy let out a yelp and with a start Jo relaxed her grip and bent to soothe it. She stroked it back to sleep, its fat little tummy and its utter trust weakening something inside her.

'How...?' she whispered when she finally dared to look at him. 'How did that come about?'

He glanced at his watch. 'Well, shoot—look at the time? Lucinda, you'd better point me in the direction of the kitchen if I'm to serve you at seven on the dot.'

He went out to his car, returning with two laden

baskets filled with the most intriguing-looking ingredients.

He grinned at Jo. 'I understand you're my kitchen
hand?'

She tried to smile back, but couldn't. 'Yay,' she
said weakly instead.

'Buck up, Jo. All I want you to do is assemble a
macaron tower.'

That was the problem. Mac didn't want her for
anything more substantial. Her fingers curled
against her palms. Why had her grandmother hired
him? And, more to the point, why had Mac agreed
to it?

They settled the puppies in their baskets in the
laundry. Mac unpacked his groceries. Jo washed
her hands and set about icing two plastic cones.

Mac glanced at them. 'Why two?'

He'd come up so close behind her his breath
raised all the fine hairs at her nape. She wanted
him to kiss her. She ached with it. But he hadn't
given her so much as a kiss on the cheek, and that
spoke volumes.

In her heart she knew it was for the best.

'I don't think I've mentioned yet what a sight for
sore eyes you are.'

She was wearing an old pair of tracksuit pants

and an oversized T-shirt that had once been blue but was now grey. She was a sight, all right, but not the kind he meant.

She spun around. 'What are you doing here, Mac?'

His gaze lowered to her mouth. Beneath tanned flesh the pulse at the base of his jaw pounded. Hunger roared through her. They swayed towards each other, but at the last moment he snapped away.

'If I kiss you now I'll be lost, and I did promise your grandmother I'd make this meal.' He ground that last from between clenched teeth. He glared at her. 'And you promised her that darn *macaron* tower.' He suddenly seized her shoulders in a strong grip. 'But after this party we're talking.'

'Right.' She swallowed. 'Good.'

Except… He wasn't going to go over old ground, was he? He wouldn't ask her to return to the beach house as his housekeeper, would he?

He had to know that wasn't enough.

His fingers tightened, although she sensed how he tempered his strength.

'What's the plan for this evening? Is there anything you'd like me to do?'

Love me.

She swallowed that back, shrugged. 'Just follow my lead, I guess. I think I have it under control.'

Fingers crossed.

They stared at each other for a long fraught moment. She swung away, her heart surging in her chest. One thing was clear—she and Mac still generated heat. Not that it made a bit of difference. Other than to make working with him in the confines of a suburban kitchen all the more fraught, uncomfortable...and exciting.

Focus on making the tower.

She'd been concentrating on this event for weeks now. She couldn't afford to let Mac derail her.

She made the *macaron* tower—carefully inserting toothpicks into the iced cones and then painstakingly attaching the coloured *macarons*. When that was done she decorated it all with swirls of pink, green and lemon ribbon.

She stood back to admire it and almost stepped on Mac.

She glanced back at him. 'What do you think?'

Ugh! Think you could sound any needier?

She tossed her head. 'It's pretty fabulous, isn't it?'

'It's beautiful.'

But he was looking at her when he said it, not at

the tower. The air between them shimmered. He took a hasty step away and Jo had to bite back the moan that rose through her.

Mac cleared his throat. 'What flavours did you decide to go with?'

She kept her gaze on the tower. 'Lime with passionfruit cream, and strawberry with a vanilla buttercream.'

'Nice.'

She picked up the tower and very *very* carefully walked it into the pantry.

Then she made a second tower, identical to the first. It was just as perfect. She set it in the pantry beside the first one.

Mac raised an eyebrow. She merely shrugged.

'Jo, dear.' Her grandmother came bustling in. 'Guests will start arriving in forty minutes and you've yet to shower and dress.'

'And take the puppies out for a pee and a romp in the back yard,' Jo added. 'Go ahead and finish getting ready, Grandma. I won't be late. I promise.'

CHAPTER TWELVE

Jo ROMPED WITH the puppies for fifteen minutes, but all the while she was aware that Mac was in her childhood home and…and…

And what?

She settled the puppies back in their baskets and went to shower. She'd splurged on a new dress for the occasion. And heels. She'd almost be the same height as Mac in them.

Almost, but not quite.

Her grandmother was shooting last-minute instructions at Mac when Jo returned to the lounge room. During her absence Great-Aunt Edith had arrived. They all broke off to stare.

Jo turned on the spot. '*Now* I'm a sight for sore eyes,' she shot at Mac.

Her dress was a simple shift in a startling geometric pattern of orange, purple and black. It stopped a couple of inches short of her knees. She'd never worn anything so short before, and certainly not with heels. She had legs that… Well, they practically went on forever—even if she did say so herself.

Mac's eyes blazed obligingly. Fire licked along her belly in instant response.

'Nice,' he croaked.

'Good Lord, Jo! What *are* you wearing?' Her great-aunt tut-tutted. 'It's far too short for a girl of your height.'

'The shop assistant assured me it was perfect for a girl of my height,' Jo countered.

'You look very pretty, Jo, dear,' her grandma said.

Great-Aunt Edith glared. 'But is it *seemly*?'

Jo glanced back at Mac, who could barely drag his gaze from her legs, and a female purr of satisfaction rose through her. 'Oh, I expect it's quite the opposite, Aunt Edith, but I believe that's the point.'

Before her aunt could remonstrate further the doorbell rang and Jo went to answer it, putting a sway into her step for Mac's benefit.

Eat your heart out.

When she returned he'd retreated to the kitchen and she could breathe easier again. He needn't think he could come around here and get her all het-up without expecting some kind of payback.

Five additional guests had been invited to dinner, all of them longstanding friends of her grand-mother's and great-aunt's—people Jo had known all her life.

Each of them stared at her as if they didn't rec-ognise her when she answered the door. They'd stare a whole lot more before she was through this evening.

She went to serve drinks, but Mac was there be-fore her.

'Who *is* that young man?' her great-aunt de-manded of her grandmother.

'Aunt Edith, this is Malcolm MacCallum—the famous chef,' Jo said. 'I was his housekeeper for a short time not that long ago.'

'Humph. I remember. I can't believe you'd waste your education on such a lowly position as house-maid.'

'What does it matter?' her grandmother piped up. 'As long as she was happy.'

Happy? Jo shoulders started to droop.

'And I can't believe you're turning your back on the possibility of promotion, not to mention stabil-ity, by switching vocations so late in life.'

Late in life? Jo choked.

Mac's lips twitched, and her great-aunt's eyes

narrowed. 'Precisely how well do you know this Malcolm?'

She made her smile bright. 'Very well.'

Great-Aunt Edith drew herself up to her full formidable height. 'I'd like to know—'

'I'm afraid it's none of your business.'

'Jo!' her grandmother remonstrated.

'Or yours either, Grandma.'

The sisters stared at each other, evidently nonplussed.

'How long before we eat?' Jo shot out of the corner of her mouth.

Mac cleared his throat. 'If everyone would like to move into the dining room, I'll serve the entrée.'

Jo silently blessed him, and moved towards the kitchen to help, but with a gentle shove he pushed her towards the dining room.

'I have it covered.'

Right. Was he ever going to tell her what Ethan was doing at his beach house? And did it have any bearing on them—him and her?

There is no you and him.

Her grandmother sat at the head of the table and her great-aunt at the foot. Her grandmother's allies sat on the right side of the table—which was where Jo found herself—and her great-aunt's ranged down the left.

Like a battlefield.

As if this were a war.

And then it started.

'Do you think it's *wise* to wear such high heels when you're such a large girl, Jo?'

'Eadie, don't be such an old-fashioned prig. Our Jo is the height of fashion.'

Everyone else around the table weighed in with an opinion.

'I think that dress and those heels are perfect,' Mac said, serving mussels in garlic sauce.'

Both sisters glared at him, united for a moment in their mutual suspicion. Jo hid a smile.

In the next instant, however, the entire table had lost themselves in the delight of the food, forgetting all about Mac. Across the table he caught her eye. He mouthed 'perfect' before disappearing back into the kitchen. Her pulse skittered. Her heart throbbed.

When everyone had finished the entrée her great-aunt said, 'Jo, I really think you need to reconsider this career change you've been talking about.'

'Oh, Eadie, stop fussing. If this is what Jo wants—and if it'll make her happy—then so be it.'

'Heavens, Lucinda—a *paramedic*? Any Tom, Dick or Harriet can train as one of those. Our Jo is better than that.'

'Your Jo is quite simply the best,' Mac said, having whisked their entrée plates away and now serving lamb so succulent it melted in the mouth.

'She'll become a drudge,' her great-aunt said.

Grandma shook her head. 'Her choice.'

'I'd quite happily become *her* drudge,' Mac said.

Jo nearly swallowed her tongue.

'Who *is* he?' her great-aunt demanded.

'He's Mac.' She had no other explanation.

'He's her admirer,' Grandma said.

'If Jo had what it took to catch a man she'd have done so years ago,' scoffed Great-Aunt Edith.

'Ha!' snapped Grandma. 'Jo has her head screwed on right. Life is far easier when one doesn't have to pander to a man. Not that *you'd* know about that, Eadie.'

Ouch! Jo winced on her aunt's behalf.

'If Jo married me I'd be a very lucky man.'

Jo's fingers tightened about her cutlery and her stomach churned. What game was Mac playing?

'If you married him you could eat like this every night,' one of her grandmother's cronies said.

They ate then, mostly in silence, all relishing the amazing food.

Eventually Great-Aunt Edith pushed her plate away. 'Ladies, don't forget to leave room for dessert.' She shot Jo a smirk. 'I take it there *will* be dessert?'

'But of course.'

'Ah, but will it be the *promised* dessert?' She folded her arms and glared down the table. 'What *I* want to know is if she's managed to pull off what she promised she could. Lucy? Did she or did she not make you a *macaron* tower?'

Her grandmother smiled benignly. 'Where are the stakes?'

Jo rolled her eyes when the contested pearls were placed with ridiculous ceremony in the middle of the table.

Mac cleared the plates. 'I'll pour the dessert wine,' he said, moving to the sideboard. 'Jo, you can bring in the dessert.'

'The dishes?' she asked him.

'All cleared.'

'The puppies?'

'Safely tucked away in the laundry.'

Good. Right. She drew in a breath, rose, and moved to the kitchen.

As carefully as she'd ever done anything in her life, Jo picked up the first tower that she'd made and backed out of the pantry. She paused outside the doorway to the dining room for a moment, to pull in a breath, and balancing carefully on her new heels entered the room.

Gasps rose up all around her.

She set the concoction in front of her grandmother and with a quiver of relief stepped back again. Mission accomplished.

'Happy birthday, Grandma. I love you.' She kissed her grandmother's cheek.

They sang 'Happy Birthday', but throughout the song she couldn't help but notice, even though Great-Aunt Edith's voice was the loudest, how her aunt's gaze kept returning to the tower in awe. And she recognised something else there too—hunger and yearning.

When the song finished Jo left the room and returned with the second tower. She set it down in front of her great-aunt. 'I made this one for you Aunt Edith, because I love you too.'

'But...' Grandma spluttered. 'It's not Eadie's birthday.'

'Maybe not, but you both deserve pretty, beautiful things. To me, you're both the most beautiful women I know, and you've helped to make me the woman I am today.'

They stared at her, but neither spoke.

'My real gift to you today, Grandma, is to bring this ridiculous feud of yours and Aunt Edith's to an end.' She reached across the table and took the pearls. 'These now belong to me. I have no cousins. It's what Great-Grandmother would've wanted. Besides…' She clasped them around her throat. 'They go perfectly with my outfit.'

The sisters' jaws dropped.

'Those towers consist of your individual favourite *macaron* flavours. The combination is perfect—much better than if they were just one or the other. Just as the two of *you* are perfect together.'

Both women's eyes had grown suspiciously damp.

'I love you. I know you both love me. I also know you love each other—even if you find the words too hard to say. Great-Aunt Edith, it's time for you to come home. This is where you belong and this is where you're wanted.'

Grandma blew her nose loudly. 'She's right, Eadie.'

Great-Aunt Edith cleared her throat—twice. 'Lucy, I can't tell you how glad I am to hear it.'

'Excellent.' Mac broke into the moment. 'Now that *that's* settled, I'm stealing Jo away.' He raised a hand before anyone could argue with him. 'She's not fond of *macarons*, so I've made her a dessert of her own.'

He took her arm.

'Jo?' her grandmother and her great-aunt said in unison.

'It's okay,' Jo said. 'I'll shout if I need rescuing.'

With that, she allowed him to pull her into the kitchen.

He turned with a grin that turned her heart over and over.

'That was masterfully done,' he said.

'Yes.' It had left her feeling powerful. 'What dessert did you make me?'

He handed her a plate. 'Pineapple upside-down cake.'

She took a mouthful and closed her eyes in bliss. When she opened them Mac was staring at her with a naked hunger he didn't try to hide. It only made her feel more powerful and assured...and bold.

She tipped up her chin. 'When are you going to tell me you love me?'

He met her gaze uncertainly. 'I thought I'd been saying it all evening.'

He had.

Her great-aunt and her grandmother came bustling into the kitchen.

'My dear, I do believe it's terribly poor form to just leave the table like that.'

'Yes—listen to your grandmother. We raised you better than that.'

'I agree. But I'm afraid there are puppies to attend to. Unless you'd rather deal with the puppies yourselves?'

'Maybe Malcolm could…?'

'Not in a caterer's job description, I'm afraid,' Mac said, edging Jo towards the back door.

'Puppies?' asked Great-Aunt Edith.

'Come along, dear, and I'll tell you about them. Malcolm brought one for me and…' she glanced at Jo '…one for you, Eadie dear.'

Grandma had just given away her puppy!

'There are more puppies back at the beach house,' Mac whispered in her ear.

Jo let out a breath. Okay.

Before Grandma and Great-Aunt Edith could form another argument, Jo took Mac's hand and led him outside.

'You left the puppies behind,' Mac said.

'But I do still have hold of my dessert.'

She released him to eat another spoonful. She took a step away from him so she could breathe and think.

She lifted her plate. 'This is divine.'

'You're divine.'

Mac stared at the woman he loved and wondered if he'd done enough to win her.

If he hadn't he'd just do more. He'd do more and more and still more if he had to—to convince her that they belonged together, to prove to her that he could make her happy.

She led him down to an old swing set and sat on the swing. He leaned against the frame and feasted his eyes on her. He burned to kiss her, but while it killed him he had no intention of hauling her into his arms until he was one hundred per cent certain it was what she wanted.

She had questions. Rightly. It was only fair that he answered them.

'You somehow managed to manipulate my grandmother into asking you to come here today?'

'Guilty as charged.'

'Because you were worried I might fail with the *macarons*?'

He had no intention of lying to her. 'I came here today to help you in whatever capacity you needed me to.'

She'd outdone herself with those *macaron* towers, though.

She pursed her lips, staring at him. 'So you worked out early on that I was trying to get Grandma and Great-Aunt Edith arguing on the same side? Against me?'

'It was a good plan. But it seemed only fair that someone should argue on your side too.'

If she'd let him, he'd always argue her case.

'Why is Ethan at your beach house?'

She sat in the moonlight, eating pineapple upside-down cake in that sexy little purple and orange number, and for a moment he couldn't speak. The urge to kiss her grew, but he tamped it down. After all this time away from her just being able to look at her thrilled him.

The night was mild for this time of year, but not exactly warm. He slipped his jacket off and settled it around her shoulders.

The flash of vulnerability in her eyes when he moved in close stabbed at him.

He eased back, his heart thumping and his mouth dry. 'Everything you said to me before you left was a hundred per cent on the money.'

He closed his eyes. What if he hadn't done enough? What if his best wasn't good enough? What if she simply wished him well and turned away? How would he cope?

'I don't want to play games, Mac.'

His eyes flew open.

She rose. 'If you don't want to talk then I'd like to go back inside.'

He was being pathetic. Spineless. Waiting for a sign from her first.

A real man wouldn't hesitate.

Earn her!

'Please don't go, Jo. I was just gathering my thoughts. It's been a crazy couple of months and I'm trying to work out where to start.'

She searched his face. Slowly she sat again. 'Tell me what happened after I left.'

He leant back against the swing set's A-frame. 'I threw myself into finishing the cookbook. I finished it in record time.'

'Congratulations.'

'And then, with nothing to keep me occupied, I had a lot of time to think.'

'Ah.'

'And some of the things you said tormented me—like trying harder where Ethan was concerned. So I started wondering what more I could do to help him.'

'And…?'

She stared up at him and her lips glistened as if she'd just moistened them. Hunger roared through him.

'It took me longer to work out than it should've.'

'And what did you work out?'

'That he needed to be shaken up the same way you shook me up.'

Her lovely mouth dropped open.

'I talked to his doctor first. I had no intention of barging in like a bull in a china shop like I did the last time. The doctor and I came up with a plan to bring him to the beach house, and then we got Diana Devlin on-side.'

'I bet that wasn't easy.'

He and Diana might never be the best of friends, but they'd come to an understanding.

'Once the doctor told her he thought it'd be for the best she was behind the plan a hundred per cent.'

Jo leaned towards him. 'How did you convince Ethan to go with you?'

'I used emotional blackmail. Just like you had on me. By the way, Russ sends his love. I'm staying with him tonight.'

'You've *seen* Russ?'

'I've seen quite a bit of Russ.'

'He's not mentioned it to me.'

Because Mac had asked him not to. He hadn't wanted to get her hopes up. He hadn't known how long things with Ethan would take.

She sagged, one hand pressed to her chest. 'I'm so glad.'

'I am too,' he said quietly. 'There are some mistakes I'm never going to make again. But back to Ethan. I told him his mother needed a holiday, but that she refused to go without him. I told him she'd fall ill if she wasn't careful.'

Her mouth hooked up. 'Nice work.'

His chest puffed out.

'And he's improving?'

'It's taken a while, but, yes. The sea air and the fact he can see how good the break has been for his mother have both worked wonders. It's the puppies, though, that have really been working magic.'

She leant back, her eyes wide. 'Wow, that's really something.'

It was. 'Every now and again he starts to talk

about the future. We even had an argument last week about what recipes I should put in my next cookbook.'

Her urgings to keep trying, not to give up, to try harder, had made a man of him. Regardless of what happened from here, he was glad—and grateful—to have known her.

'He doesn't blame me for the accident, Jo. He's learning not to blame himself either.'

She set her now empty plate on the ground and rose to stand in front of him. 'That's wonderful news.'

His heart started to race. Hard.

'He still has a way to go. There'll be more skin grafts down the track. But eventually he'll be able to return to work. When he's ready I mean to help him any way I can.'

She moved another inch closer. Mac swallowed, his hands clenching at his sides.

'I don't know—' His voice cracked. 'I don't know if you can live with that. You might see it as me putting him first.'

She shook her head. 'I see it as you being a good friend—a true friend. I certainly don't see it as a sacrifice or self-immolation or a sign of guilt.'

He stared at her. 'That's good, right?'

'That's very good.'

He couldn't drag his gaze from the smoky depths of her eyes. Was she saying what he thought she was saying?

He seized her face in his hands, unable to resist the need to touch her. 'What are you saying, Jo?'

No, wait!

'No, wait,' he said. 'Let me tell you what *I'm* saying. I'm saying I love you, my beautiful girl.' He brushed her hair back from her face. 'I'm saying I want a life with you. I'm saying that fighting for you—by fighting to work out the right thing to do where Ethan was concerned—has made a man of me. I'm saying that if you give me a chance I will prove to you every single day that you are my first, foremost and most cherished priority.'

His hands moved back to cup her face.

'You are my number one, Jo. Please say you'll let me prove it.'

She pressed a hand to his lips. Her face came in close to his, her eyes shining and her lips trembling. 'I love you, Mac,' she whispered.

He wanted to punch the air. He wanted to whirl her around in his arms. He wanted to kiss her.

'No man has ever made me believe in myself the way you have. No man has made me feel so desired or so beautiful or so right.' She swallowed. 'Yes, please. I really want the chance to build a life with you.'

He stared down into her face as every dream he'd been too afraid to dream lay before him in a smorgasbord of promise.

Jo's eyes started to dance. She leaned in so close her words played across his lips. 'This is the part where you kiss me.'

He didn't wait another second, but swooped down to seize her lips in a kiss that spoke of all he couldn't put into words. He kissed her with his every pent-up hope and fear, with the joy and frustration that had shaken through him these last months since he'd met her. And she kissed him back with such ardent eagerness and generosity it eased the burn in his soul.

He lifted his head with a groan, gathering her in close. 'I love you, Jo. I nearly went crazy when I thought I'd lost you.'

Her arms tightened about him. 'You haven't lost me. I'm in your arms, where I belong, and I'm not planning on going anywhere.'

'You mean that?'

'With all my heart.'

And then she frowned. 'Well, I mean, I *do* start

my paramedic training next week, so I'll have to leave your arms literally, but you know what I mean.'

He dropped a kiss to the tip of her nose. Her very cute nose. 'But you'll keep returning here? To me?'

Her fingers stroked his nape. 'There's nowhere I'd rather be,' she whispered.

'I can commute between the coast and Sydney,' he said.

'And I can commute between Sydney and the coast,' she said. 'But, Mac, we need to make sure that wherever we go we always have room for friends and for puppies.'

A grin started up inside him until it bubbled from him in a laugh. 'I'm glad you feel that way, because Bandit had ten of the little beggars.'

Her mouth dropped open, so he kissed her again. When he lifted his head—much, *much* later—she smiled dreamily up at him.

'Did I mention that I happen to love the way you kiss?'

'No.'

So she proceeded to tell him. Which meant, of course, that he had to kiss her again.

When he lifted his head this time he found himself growling, 'Promise me forever.'

She reached up to press her hand to his cheek. 'I promise you, Mac—' she stared deep into his eyes '—that for as long as you make me pineapple upside-down cake, I'm yours. Forever.'

Her voice washed over him like warm honey and he started to laugh…and it filled his soul.

* * * * *